Before the Storm

Sean McMullen is one of Australia's leading SF and fantasy authors, with fourteen books and sixty stories published, for which he has won over a dozen awards. His most recent novels are *The Ancient Hero* (2004) and *Voidfarer* (2006). In the late 1990s he established himself in the American market, and his work has been translated into Polish, French, Japanese and other languages. The settings for Sean's work range from the Roman Empire, through Medieval Europe, to cities of the distant future. His work is a mixture of romance, invention and adventure, while populated by dynamic, strange and often hilarious characters. When not writing he is a computer training manager, and when not at a keyboard he is a karate instructor.

Also by Sean McMullen

The Centurion's Empire
Souls in the Great Machine
The Miocene Arrow
Eyes of the Calculor
The Ancient Hero (The Quentaris Chronicles)
Voyage of the Shadowmoon
Glass Dragons
Voidfarer

BEFORE THE STORM

Sean McMullen

FORD ST

First published by Ford Street Publishing, an imprint of
Hybrid Publishers, PO Box 52, Ormond VIC 3204

Melbourne Victoria Australia

© Sean McMullen 2007

2 4 6 8 10 9 7 5 3 1

First published 2007

National Library of Australia Cataloguing-in-
Publication data:

McMullen, Sean, 1948- .

Before the storm.

ISBN 9781876462505 (pbk.).

I. Title.

A823.3

Cover design & photography by Grant Gittus Graphics
Sara and Tom clothed by Malcolm's Costume Hire,
Collingwood VIC.

Printed in Australia by McPherson's Printing Group

CONTENTS

PROLOGUE

FoxS3 cowered in the darkness, and there was such silence around him that he believed he had lost his hearing. It was as if someone had slammed a door on the battle where he had been only a moment earlier. The air had the reek of rotting things, and even this was beyond his experience. The smell of charred bodies was nothing unusual to a warrior cadet like Fox, but in all of his short life he had never smelled rotting vegetables. He was still holding his wounded commander, BC, and had a plasma lance rifle slung over his shoulder. He removed his sunglasses, and as his eyes adjusted to the gloom he saw that he was in a narrow alleyway.

Now the sound of something else beyond Fox's experience caught his attention. Warily he lay the unconscious BC down and thumbed his plasma rifle into life. As his finger began to squeeze the trigger, a horse clopped past in the street beyond the alley's entrance, pulling a carriage filled with people who were laughing and singing. FoxS3 flicked the energy weapon off, feeling vaguely foolish, then he suddenly realised that there was nothing wrong with his hearing. There was no background rumble of a city jammed solid with machines. This was a city with very few machines.

Fox checked BC, who was breathing but still unconscious. Setting the rifle's target laser to broadview, he lit up the alley. It was filled with rubbish bins, broken barrels, shards of glass from smashed bottles, and wind-blown newspapers. The dates of the newspapers spanned several weeks, but all had the same year in common: 1901. Fox switched off the light and melted into the shadows at the sound of approaching voices.

A man paused at the entrance to the alley, glanced about, then entered. Adrenaline burned through Fox as he prepared to drop the intruder silently. That would conserve energy in the plasma rifle's power lattice. The man fumbled with his trousers, then began to urinate against a wall. Fox again felt extremely foolish. Two more men stopped at the entrance to the alley.

'Oi, George, would ya be pointin' the poker in there?' called one of them.

'Away with ya, give a man some peace,' George shouted back.

'Now fancy doin' a thing like that!' called the third man. 'Fortnight a-fore Melbourne becomes capital of Australia, an' what does he do? He pisses on it.'

'Yeah, no respect for the first Australian parliament,' called his companion.

'Parliament's not to be meetin' in this alley,' George replied as he walked out, buttoning his fly. 'Shake a leg now, or we'll miss the last train.'

'Aren't you gonna wash yer hands?'

'Didn't piss on 'em.'

As the voices faded into the distance Fox heard the faintest of gasps as BC returned to consciousness.

'Fox, to me!' the young commander hissed in the darkness.

'Reporting!' Fox responded.

'Status?'

'Timejump, on target. Night, April, 1901.'

There was a short silence while the wounded student-commander grasped the implications of the words.

'NineFive, in future, still!' BC panted.

'On target,' said Fox.

'Fox, order, mark!' said BC urgently. 'NineFive, prevent.'

Fox considered the brief order carefully, not because he was slow-witted, but because it was so very important.

'Order, NineFive, prevent, verifying,' he whispered steadily.

'Lockdown,' said BC.

'Lockdown,' echoed Fox, confirming that he understood the most important order in all of Earth's history.

1

SOLDIER

The Lang children went boating on the Yarra River every Saturday afternoon during summer and autumn. While their father was at the Melbourne Club, and his wife met her friends for tea and cakes at a nearby café, Emily and Daniel would hire a boat and glide up and down the river among the racing shells of the school crews training for the regattas later in the year. It was a family tradition that was only three years old, but for Emily and her brother it seemed like they had been doing it forever.

On this particular afternoon there were artists on the bank. The thought crossed Emily's mind that the scene might soon become some famous painting, and that their boat would be included.

Daniel had the gangly, stretched look of someone who had recently grown too fast, and while Emily had the figure of a woman, she still had to wear her long, auburn hair brushed out like a girl. The artists might have waited until Daniel and she had grown up a little more, but she decided to make the most of it.

'Look your best, Danny, people are painting us to-day,' she said as she straightened her straw hat, then leaned back in the bow of the boat to let her hand trail in the water.

'Artists?' he asked, looking about. 'Where?'

'On the south bank, near the boatsheds. They are probably painting the river, with St Paul's Cathedral in the background.'

'What a boring picture,' replied Daniel. He then shipped the oars, removed one from its lock, and stood up in the stern. Predictably, the boat began to wobble.

'Danny!' cried Emily. 'What are you doing? Sit down!'

'They need something interesting on the river, not just a rowboat,' he laughed as he dipped the end of the oar into the water. 'Now they can paint a gondola and a gondolier, Australian style.'

'Daniel! The boat's starting to rock, it's … Danny!'

It was too late. The boat rocked sharply. Daniel dropped his weight to the other side, but only succeeded in rocking it more violently in the other direction. He grabbed at the side as he fell out, pulling the boat right over to capsize on top of them.

That was as much as Emily saw for some moments. There was the shock of cold water, no air to breathe, water slowing her every move, muted sounds, dim light and then she was back at the surface. She spluttered, shrieked and sank again, then her hand brushed against the upturned rowboat. She grasped at the slippery, painted wood, got a grip on the keel, managed to get her head above the surface, then coughed water and screamed. Her fingers began to slip on the slime-covered keel of the rowboat.

Daniel was nowhere to be seen, but on the bank there were people shouting and waving. While a group tried to launch another boat, Emily saw someone take off his coat, run down the bank and dive into the water. She lost her grip on the keel, then managed to grasp it again. There was still no sign of Daniel. She called his name over and over, between calls for help. Her fingers aching, Emily lost her hold on the keel yet again. She sank. For a moment she was suspended beneath the surface, with no idea of up or down. Everything was suddenly serene, and she felt oddly calm, and then a strong hand grasped her arm. Emily spluttered water as her head broke the surface.

'Breathing, Miss?' called Emily's rescuer as she gulped for breath.

'My brother!' she gasped. 'Save Danny.'

'Swimming, you can?'

'No, but …'

'My shirt, holding. I swim.'

Emily had been towed most of the way to the bank before she realised that she was going to be safe. The youth with the oddly precise, clipped foreign accent was very strong, and swam like a champion. Ahead of them she could see people wading into the water and holding out their arms.

'My brother, he's back there,' she gasped between mouthfuls of air and water.

'Returning, rescue, for purpose of,' called the youth.

Suddenly there were hands grasping Emily and people shouting instructions and questions. A man in a dark coat with a cigar clenched between his teeth lifted Emily from the water and began wading for the bank while others gathered around, mostly asking if she was all right. She was put down on grass, and a picnic blanket was wrapped around her. A woman came running up with a wooden folding seat, but Emily tried to push those holding her away.

'My brother!' she panted. 'Danny was in the boat, too.'

Several voices answered her.

'The boat's still floating.'

'That boy's reached the boat.'

'Can't see anyone else.'

'He's dived.'

'Been down a long time.'

'There's a head.'

'It's just the lad who rescued the girl.'

'He's dived again.'

Emily pushed her way through the crowd around her in time to see the youth surface, then dive a third time. The wavelets died away, and there was nothing to be seen except for the upturned boat.

It was at this point that Emily's mother returned. The sight of Emily drenched and muddy, and everyone pointing to the upturned boat in the middle of the river, told Mrs Lang what had happened in an instant. She shrieked, ran over to Emily, hugged her daughter convulsively for a moment, then tried to rush into the river in search of her son. She was seized by several men and dragged back to the grassy bank. Emily noticed that she had lost one shoe.

'Sixty seconds down,' said a man holding a pocket watch.

'That's a long time,' said another.

'Where's that other boat?'

'They can't find the oars.'

'Gad, Sir, they can paddle with their hands.'

'There's schoolboys in a racing shell, they're coming over to help.'

'What can they do? The two lads have sunk.'

'Murky water.'

'Ninety seconds.'

'The other lad's been down five minutes, there's no hope.'

'There he is! Ninety-seven seconds and there's another head! He got him!'

Emily managed to stay on her feet long enough to see the boys in the racing shell start to tow her brother and their rescuer in the direction of the bank, then she collapsed back into the arms of those around her. She was guided back to the folding chair. There was more splashing as men waded out into the muddy water to get her brother ashore. Again she could see nothing, but the babble of voices painted a picture for her.

'What's your name, son?'

'Fox Essthree, Sir!' the boy replied in a staccato, almost military, patter.

'That was very brave of you, Fox.'

'The other boy looks gone.'

'There's a cut on his head.'

'The boat must have hit him when it capsized.'

'Get him on the bank.'

'My Danny!' shrieked Mrs Lang above the other voices.

'On his side.'

'On his back.'

'On his stomach.'

'Let me through, I'm a doctor.'

'He was down for five minutes and thirty seconds, I timed it.'

'No breathing.'

'No pulse.'

Now Emily screamed Daniel's name and surged out of the folding chair. She struggled past the other onlookers in time to see her rescuer pushing a man in a top hat away from Daniel's body. He knelt beside him. The youth had neatly cut hair and was heavily muscled, without being solidly built. Even at a distance Emily could see that his eyes were intensely blue. He was tall enough to pass for a man.

'Get back there, lad, have some respect for the dead,' said a man wearing a frock coat and a straw boating hat, who then tried to drag the youth away.

There was a brief struggle, and for a moment Emily saw the man having his arm twisted up behind his back. His mouth gaped open in either shock or pain, then the youth pushed him away. The man went stumbling off down the bank and into the shallows.

'You, doctor, pulse, monitor!' barked the youth, pointing at the doctor as he returned to kneel beside Daniel.

Something about the youth's manner had established his authority over the crowd by now. He rolled Daniel on his back, checked his pulse, then pressed down about a dozen times on his chest with the heels of his palms. Next he pulled Daniel's jaw down and breathed into it twice. Again he pumped at Daniel's chest. The voices began again, but this time they were hushed and hesitant.

'What's he doing?'

'Can't say I know.'

'It's a Hindu trick. I once saw a yogi buried alive for three days when I was in India.'

'The boy's dead!'

'Seven minutes and fifteen seconds without a breath.'

'A pulse!' shouted the doctor.

The youth sat back, then Daniel coughed. The crowd gasped with amazement, then cheered loudly. Emily fainted.

When Emily revived she could hear her mother's voice calling Daniel's name over and over. With the help of the woman who had brought the folding chair, Emily went over to where Mrs Lang was embracing her limp but living son. The youth named Fox Essthree was standing nearby, his coat over his shoulders and his arms folded. After some moments of embraces and tears with Emily, Mrs Lang demanded to know what had happened.

'Our boat capsized, and Master Essthree swam out to rescue us,' said Emily, pointing to the youth even though she knew it was rude to point. 'He pulled me ashore, then went back for Danny. He is awfully brave.'

For a moment there was silence. Several dozen pairs of eyes turned to Fox, who still stood with his arms tightly folded, shivering.

'Accident, observed,' said Fox in his soft voice and unfamiliar accent. 'Rescue, performed.'

'Daniel was *dead*, but you brought him back to life!' babbled Emily breathlessly.

'I swear it's true,' said the man who said he was a doctor. 'He had no pulse whatever, and was not breathing.'

'Status, dying, not dead,' explained Fox, looking embarrassed. 'Revival, procedure, I performed.'

'Gad, Sir!' exclaimed the doctor. 'I'm a physician, and I've not heard of such a thing.'

Fox shrugged, then stared at the ground. The doctor had authority, yet Fox had revived Daniel.

'The Chinese do things like that,' called someone.

'Chinese?' exclaimed the doctor. 'Nothing good ever came out of China!'

Still Fox said nothing. Daniel coughed and shook his head. Emily put her arms around her brother.

'Well, you never know with those Chinese,' conceded the doctor. 'Somebody fetch a hot drink for these young people, else they will catch a chill.'

Someone handed Emily a mug of hot chocolate. She sipped at it once, then the doctor took her temperature with a glass thermometer and peered down her throat. One of the schoolboys from the rowing shell found Mrs Lang's lost shoe and returned it to her. A policeman arrived, asked what the fuss was about, then made some notes in his book. A journalist from *The Argus* asked whether anyone had drowned, then seemed to lose interest when told that both Emily and Daniel had been rescued. Mrs Lang gave a florin to each of the boys from the rowing shell, and gave ten shillings to Fox. Finally the doctor offered to take Mrs Lang and her children home in his pony gig.

'And, ah, have you been long in Melbourne, Fox?' Mrs Lang asked Fox, who had been standing by quietly and saying nothing.

'Arrival, recent,' replied Fox.

'Your accent sounds foreign, but I can't place it. Definitely not French, German, or …'

'Norwegian, I'll wager,' said a man behind Emily.

Fox frowned slightly, and seemed to think carefully for a moment.

'Norwegian, I am,' he replied.

'Thought so!' exclaimed the man. 'Damn fine sailors.'

'Able seaman, first class, ranking, mine, Sir!' declared Fox, snapping to attention with his left foot slightly back and his fists held as if he were presenting a rifle across his chest.

Even Emily had been to enough parades to know that Fox's salute was not even remotely like anything done on British ships.

'Ah, so you are a sailor, then?' asked Mrs Lang.

'Sailor, formerly, ma'am! Status, discharged. Employment, local, seeking.'

It was soon established that Fox had arrived in Melbourne that same day, that his baggage had been stolen, and that he had lost his papers during the rescue.

'Oh you poor boy, and now your clothes have been soaked!' cried Mrs Lang. 'What are you to do? You simply *must* come home with us!'

Brighton was six miles south of the river, and the doctor drove his gig down St Kilda Road with his four passengers crammed onto a seat designed for two. Emily noticed that Fox looked about continually, and seemed confused and puzzled. Suddenly he stared to the left.

'Imperial War Academy!' he exclaimed softly.

'No, that's Wesley College,' said Daniel. 'I go to school there.'

Fox glanced about nervously, said, 'Mistaken,' then sat back and put a hand to his head.

'There, there, Fox, the excitement has confused you,' said Mrs Lang soothingly. 'You will be back to your old self after a hot bath and a good dinner.'

By the time the Lang family got home it was late in the afternoon. The maid was told to start a fire in the living room grate, and to boil water for three baths. Emily bathed quickly, then dressed while the maid emptied the tub. She entered the living room to find Daniel and Fox sitting with her mother, both wrapped in blankets.

'Next, you are,' said Fox to Daniel as he caught sight of Emily.

'Oh, that is very kind of you young man, but *you* are the guest,' insisted Mrs Lang.

'Being wet, am often,' replied Fox. 'Daniel, needs, more urgent.'

Mrs Lang left the room with Daniel, calling to the maid to fetch dry clothes for him.

'I would be dead were it not for you,' said Emily awkwardly.

'To rescue, my honour,' replied Fox.

'You probably think us so pitiful.'

'Why?'

'Daniel not knowing how to swim, and me able to do nothing but scream. He stood up in the boat, you know. I think it was just to tease me.'

'Myself, money, home, have none. Rescuing, myself, you are.'

'Why Fox, that is a very sweet way to put it.'

Mrs Lang returned with her sleeves still rolled up. She collapsed into an armchair and put a hand to her forehead.

'Fox, I do apologise again for keeping you waiting in wet clothes, but as you can see, my children are, well, frail compared to someone like you.'

'Acknowledged.'

'And you were a sailor …' began Mrs Lang, then she realised that all her small talk about sailors was about how rough and dirty they were. 'I … saw sailors at work on the voyage out here,' she finally managed. 'You … are the first sailor I have spoken to, however.'

'Impression, satisfactory, perhaps?' replied Fox.

'Oh indeed. A good impression, a wonderful impression. But tell me, young Fox, you seem very well spoken, and, ah, well-mannered for a sailor.'

'Acknowledged, ah, on target.'

Odd, he does not seem to know how to express his thanks to people, thought Emily.

'And your family?' asked Mrs Lang.

'Family? No target.'

'Your mother and father, your parents.'

'Kensington hatchery.'

'Ah, they were poultry farmers? But Kensington does not sound like a Norwegian name.'

For a moment Fox looked really tense, and he frowned slightly in thought.

'Ship sank, all died,' he declared, as if he wished to terminate the subject.

'Oh, I am so, so sorry!' exclaimed Mrs Lang with genuine horror, swaying a little, as if about to faint. 'How terrible. But how did you survive?'

'Can swim.'

'Ah, now it all makes sense!'

'So when you saw Daniel and me in difficulties, it reminded you of how your own parents died?' asked Emily.

Fox gave her an uneasy, deferential glance.

'Parents, yes,' he replied, nodding slightly.

'Such a fine young man, and all alone in the world,' said Mrs Lang, dabbing at one eye with a handkerchief. 'Well, perhaps *we* can be a family to you, Fox.'

'Family?' asked Fox. 'You?'

'Yes. You simply must accept our help while you
get your life in order. You could visit us here, and
play with Emily and Daniel.'

'Play?' asked Fox, as if he had never heard the
word.

'Oh goodness, you really have lost your child-
hood,' said Mrs Lang. 'Never mind, first things first.
You must have a bath, and while your clothes are
being scrubbed and dried, you can wear something
from Daniel's wardrobe and have dinner with us.'

Daniel called out that he was done with the bathroom, and now Mrs Lang sent Emily to have the
maid bring more hot water and dry towels. Fox and
Daniel were roughly the same height, so the fit of
Daniel's clothes was not much of a problem.

With the change of clothes and the towels under
her arm, Emily burst into the bathroom … to be
confronted by Fox already undressed and sitting up
in the bath. Emily saw lurid red stripes criss-crossing
his back. He looked around as Emily gasped.

'I … I brought you a towel, and, um, clothes,' she
stammered, so mortified and embarrassed that she
stood frozen to the spot. 'Danny's clothes.'

Fox nodded, his face blank. 'Thank you, Miss.'

Suddenly Emily realised that the strange, striped
pattern on his back was not an undershirt.

'Fox, your back!' she exclaimed.

'Scars, Miss.'

'But how?'

'Flogged, I was.'

There was a brief silence as the words registered with Emily. Flogged. That was something that only happened to sailors who misbehaved.

'I, um, yes, flogged,' she managed. 'That happens to sailors. I've read of it in Danny's adventure books. I'm not supposed to read adventure books, so I do it in secret.'

'Floggings, happen,' said Fox.

'But you're a child … well, a youth, that is, a young man. I mean, like Daniel.'

'Discipline, on ships, strict.'

'Goodness,' whispered Emily, still staring at the scars. 'What did you do?'

'Insolence. Fifty lashes.'

'Fifty! Goodness. You must be awfully brave. Daniel once got six strokes of the cane at school, he could not sit down without a cushion for days. How old were you when it happened?'

'Fifteen.'

'I … goodness! Fifteen. My goodness, I'm so sorry.'

'Apologies, not required.'

Suddenly remembering that she was alone with a naked youth, Emily snatched up Fox's wet clothes and backed out, then pulled the bathroom door closed behind her. For some moments she stood very still with her back to the door. Fox had been flogged while the same age as Daniel.

'Three reporting, serial K37WCB0542. Trans.'

The words had come from within the bathroom, and the voice belonged to Fox.

'Accident, boating, saved children. Maintenance facilities, courtly family, offered. Feeding, also. Currency, supplied, shillings, ten. Supplies, medical, available. Returning, estimate, twenty-two hundred. Trans.'

Another pause. It was as if Fox were talking to someone at the other end of one of the speaking tubes like they had in the big emporium stores.

'Status, neutral. Status, self? Trans.'

Emily remembered that Fox had referred to himself as Three. There was definitely something military about him, she was also sure of that.

'Understood. Trans end,' concluded Fox.

Emily waited until she heard the bath water begin to splash again before she tiptoed away.

Emily felt very self-conscious as she emptied the pockets of Fox's clothes. The fact that there was something very, very odd about him made her curious to know more about who he was, but it felt like spying and nice girls were not supposed to do that sort of thing. The pocket of his shirt contained a silvery thing about the size of a pen, but there was no nib. In his trouser pockets were a few coins, a handkerchief with IWA embroidered on it, and some type of clasp knife. His jacket pockets were empty, but in three places there were faint, brownish singes in the violet material, as if someone had pressed the tip of a red-hot poker into the cloth for a moment. The jacket had a double row of silver buttons with some sort of crest embossed on them. Emily bundled everything into the damp handkerchief, but as she picked up the trousers again, her fingers felt something else in a hidden pocket. She took it out.

The thing was like a block of smooth, black rubber, trailing black cords and inset with coloured glass that looked like jewels. The word 'Sony' was embossed in silver along one side. A *Sony*? she thought, feeling that the name might apply to a toy. She began to examine it, turning it over in her fingers. One of the tiny jewels clicked as she touched it, and a bright light flared in Emily's face. She dropped the device on the table in front of her.

A patch of light about a yard square lit up the blank wall beside the table, and it suddenly became a moving picture like in the new cinemas … except that this picture was in colour, and sounds were coming from somewhere within the Sony. Emily stood frozen with astonishment.

On the wall, images of young soldiers in violet and black uniforms like Fox's were dashing about. They were carrying short, stubby rifles that shot fire with a squeaking, hissing sound, like a cork being drawn across a bottle. The scene was a blur of flashing lights, running figures, bodies, blood, smoke and flames. Voices shouted orders in the same clipped, precise English that Fox used, and the soldiers referred to each other as numbers. The leader was a thin but stunningly handsome youth with dark hair. There was a long cut down the right side of his forehead, and it was bleeding.

For all the smoke, confusion, blood and death before her eyes, the sight of the youth that the others kept calling BC drew Emily's eyes more than anything else. He shouted the precise orders, led the way, and sprayed fire from his strange rifle as they ran. Dark figures appeared at the end of a corridor, figures that fired pretty sparkles of light that began to cut down BC's soldiers. BC stood his ground, shooting back at the attackers as one more of those beside him fell.

'Squad! Go! I cover!' he barked, then there was a bright flash and he fell, still shooting. Someone else charged past him, there was a blast of fire, then all was silent.

Emily suddenly realised that she was watching the scene from the perspective of someone who was one of BC's own soldiers. It was like the time she had acted in a school play, watching the story as one of the characters would see it. This was definitely no play, however. The watcher glanced about, saw nobody else standing, then hurried through the swirling smoke to where BC lay.

'Three, go!' cried BC, clutching his bleeding stomach.

Three! Emily remembered from the conversation heard through the bathroom door that Fox had called himself Three. Three. Fox Essthree? FoxS3? Three bent over BC, who tried to push him away with bloodied hands. Although contorted with pain and smeared with blood and soot, his face was still strangely handsome, almost beautiful.

'Leave me!' cried BC. 'Temporan machine, plan follow, NineFive, prevent.'

'Bombs set,' shouted Fox's voice. 'Temporan machine, for two, have configured!'

'Leave me, am dying!' cried BC.

'Timeslip, in three, detonation, in five!' replied FoxS3. 'One, two, three!'

The scene suddenly changed to the words 'battery low', then winked out.

Drained, shaken, unsteady on her feet, and fighting the urge to be sick, Emily added the device to what was bundled in the handkerchief. Next she rushed off to the toilet and vomited up her lunch, the mug of chocolate, and some river water. She was washing her face in a hand basin when the maid arrived.

'Yer father's 'ome, Miss Emily, and young Danny's telling him rare, wild stories 'bout Master Fox an' the rescue,' she warned.

'I shall go to him too, Martha. Now here are

Master Fox's clothes. Wash them quickly, and put them in the drying cabinet.'

'They'll be hours dryin', Miss. Ooh aye! Expensive-lookin' threads, the young master has.'

'He is a sailor,' replied Emily, confused by the maid's opinion.

'Odd cut about 'em, too. I reckon 'e's an officer.'

'He has just recently arrived, on a foreign ship. They must dress like that in, um, Norway.'

''Ere, there's no buttons on 'is trousers! Only ... well, they looks like little teeth.'

'Just get along and wash them, Martha!'

Emily picked up the things wrapped in the handkerchief and made her way to the bathroom. Reaching the door, she hesitated for a moment as something nagged at the back of her mind. She examined the coins again. There were ten shillings in florins, all from the 1890s. An 1897 sixpence looked familiar enough, as did the pennies and halfpennies. She picked out another silver coin, stared at the writing, then very nearly dropped it in surprise. The writing on it declared the monarch to be Charles III. Was Charles the king of Norway? Emily wondered. At that moment there was a clack from the latch of the bathroom door. She dropped the coin back into the handkerchief as Fox emerged. Emily blinked in surprise to see someone else wearing her brother's clothes.

'Um, Master Fox, I emptied your pockets before

giving your things to the maid to wash!' she stammered as Fox stopped before her.

'Thanks, to you, Miss,' Fox replied softly, as he accepted the little bundle.

❁

Over dinner, it was Mr Lang's turn to question Fox about his background.

'And how did you survive the shipping accident that claimed your family?' he asked.

'Can swim,' Fox reiterated.

'Ah, quite so, quite so. And now you are alone in the world, as my dear wife and I would have been were it not for you. How do you cope with the sadness?'

'Training,' replied Fox simply. 'Was distraction.'

'Quite so, sensible attitude. Bit of a jog around the football field does wonders to clear the mind and lift the gloom, what? Do it myself. Now, what about work? I could have a word to old Aitkinson, the grocer. He needs a smart boy to do deliveries. Can you ride a bike?'

'Norton 750CC, cadet standard, liaison class, all-terrain …' began Fox, before he suddenly caught himself and forced his face into a blank expression.

'A bike, lad, a bicycle. Two wheels, you pedal, it moves.'

'Cycle!' exclaimed Fox in relief. 'Yes, cycle, for use, am trained.'

'Ah, good, good. Now look here, Fox, I think that the best course is for you to work for old Aitkinson for a few weeks, delivering groceries. It will earn you some shillings to get by while you look around for a proper apprenticeship, so that you can better yourself. Where are you staying?'

'Room, in hostelry.'

'Ah, splendid, but there is a spare room here, bear that in mind. What profession takes your fancy?'

'Electricity, is future.'

'Electricity, eh? Smart lad, smart lad. Good prospects in electricity. But you know, I've been thinking. You could do better.'

'Better?'

Mr Lang got up and walked over to the mantelpiece, above which several guns were mounted. He selected a stubby pistol.

'David!' exclaimed his wife. 'Keep that horrible thing away from the dinner table.'

'Please dear, there is no need for formality,' Mr Lang said as he held the pistol out to Fox. 'What can you tell me about this, young man?'

Fox took the weapon and examined it briefly.

'Lancaster, 1882, thirty-eight calibre, four barrels, brake action striker, unjammable, effective usage, close quarters.'

There was a short silence.

'Astounding,' breathed Mr Lang. 'All perfectly correct. And tell me, Fox, what is its use?'

'Circumstances, extreme danger, when needed quickly, fire with certainty, close range.'

'Yes, yes, all quite correct. I knew it! You have an interest in weapons. You are as brave as a lion, as fit as a bull, and you have a natural military bearing about you. Young man, you should consider a career in the army. Once you are a British citizen why, you could become a captain in no time at all.'

'Army, Sir?' responded Fox suspiciously.

'Oh yes! You have an education, in spite of your halting English. That's a big plus next to your name. Mind you, people need connections to get ahead in today's military, but I have those connections. It would be the British army, mind, no future in our stupid little colonial militias. You would have to go to England, but I know people who know people.'

'Am grateful,' replied Fox with deference. 'Your offer, shall consider.'

After dinner Mr Lang retired to his study, and Mrs Lang sat with Fox and her children in the living room, before the fire.

'Fox, would you really go to England and join the army?' asked Emily as she stared into the hot coals.

'If ordered, Miss.'

'But you are not on your ship now, there is nobody to order you to do anything.'

Fox looked as if he were about to say something,

then frowned. 'Correct,' he conceded. 'Habit, discipline, persisting.'

'Your speech really is very precise and, well, military sounding,' observed Mrs Lang.

'At sea, years,' replied Fox slowly. 'Ship discipline, like military.'

'You are wonderfully well spoken for a foreigner, even if you do sound a little formal,' said Emily. 'What are you interested in?'

Fox froze for a moment. 'History. Natural philosophy.'

Suddenly Emily realised that Fox never said 'um', 'ah', or 'er'. He thought about what he had been asked, his face blank, then he replied.

'Oh I know all about natural philosophy,' said Daniel, pleased to discover something in common with his rescuer. 'Can you name the planets?'

'Mercury, Venus, Earth, Mars, asteroids, Jupiter, Saturn, Uranus, Neptune, the double planet Charon and Cerebus, and Terminus.'

'Gosh!' exclaimed the youth.

'Daniel!' his mother exclaimed. 'Language, please! Fox, I can tell the maid to prepare the bed in the garret for you. Would you like to stay here for the night? You must be exhausted.'

'My thanks, no.'

'Daniel, kindly show Fox to his room … oh! Sorry, did you say no?'

'Tonight, expected, at lodgings. Friends, worried, will be.'

'Oh. I see. Well, ah, would you come here for lunch tomorrow? We have a roast on Sundays, you would love it. We might even be able to give you introductions to people, you know, help you become established in Melbourne.'

Fox considered this carefully before answering. It was not yet late in the evening, but the last train was due soon.

'Shall return, tomorrow, if clothing wet.'

Half an hour later Fox went to the laundry with Mrs Lang, to check on the progress with drying his clothes. Daniel had already been out of the room for some time. Emily and Daniel had spent their lives reading about heroes in the classics that they studied at school, and in adventure novels. Now they had actually met one, and he had rescued them. Fox was everything that a hero should be, as far as Emily was concerned: brave, strong, well-mannered, modest, yet ... there was something very strange about him. His manner was distant and withdrawn, like that of a dog that had been beaten too often, and had learned to avoid trouble. He was highly intelligent, yet he took a lot of care to disguise the fact. He said nothing funny, and even missed jokes made by others. Fox did laugh, but only when others were laughing. Emily felt sure that the mistakes he made were not really those of a foreigner. Try as she might, however, she could not think of anyone that he resembled.

As Emily sat staring into the fire, she found herself daydreaming about BC. Annoyed with herself, she switched her thoughts to Fox. Moments later her thoughts drifted back to BC. He was shooting at dark shapes in the smoke, his skin pale, and his hair dark and wavy. Again Emily tried to think about Fox. It was he who had rescued her, after all. Moments later she found herself dreaming about nursing the wounded BC back to health. Slowly the day began to catch up with Emily, and she caught herself starting to doze. Daniel came back into the room with a book.

'I was just checking what Fox said about the names of the planets,' her brother announced. 'He got them right, except that he put in three make-believe names at the end.'

Once again something unsettling began batting about like a moth at the back of Emily's mind. She shivered.

'Can I see?' she asked as casually as she could.

'Yes, but be quick about it. You know how Mother and Father feel about girls learning science.'

Emily quickly turned to the book's chapter on astronomy. She was surprised to learn that some planets had not always been known. Uranus had been discovered in 1781, and Neptune in 1846. There were many asteroids, but the first had only been discovered in 1801. Charon, Cerebus and

Terminus were definitely not mentioned.

'Tomorrow's Sunday,' said Daniel. 'You know what we do on Sunday?'

'We go to church, have a roast for lunch, then spend the rest of the day being bored.'

'Well, I think that if Fox's clothes are not dry, he might have to come back for them. If he returns early, he could come to church with us before lunch. Mother did invite him … well, sort of.'

'Why not ask him, silly?'

' It … it sounds, er, sissy, a boy asking another boy to go to church. I thought you might ask him instead.'

'No!' exclaimed Emily. 'He might think that I had, ah, an *interest* in him. Danny, just make the suggestion yourself.'

'But only girls make those sorts of suggestions.'

'Oh, nonsense.'

'I still think a girl should ask that sort of thing.'

'No!'

'Look, why don't we both ask him? That way I don't look like a sissy, and you don't look like you're courting him.'

Emily considered this. Push Daniel too far, and he would drop the subject. Daniel clearly wanted to be more of a friend to Fox, while Emily was intrigued by him. Now Daniel was offering a compromise. With careful, casual questioning, Fox might talk about BC, and the very thought of that quickened Emily's pulse.

'I'll go with you, but only if you actually speak to him,' she conceded.

'Can I say that it was your idea?' asked Daniel eagerly.

'You can say it was *our* idea,' Emily said firmly.

'I suppose that will have to do … but I still say boys are not supposed to ask other boys to church. Girls do that sort of thing.'

'Fox was brave enough to rescue us, so you must be brave enough to ask him to church.'

The mention of bravery changed everything as far as Daniel was concerned.

'All right, all right, I'll do it.'

Just then they heard Fox returning from the laundry with Mrs Lang.

'I cannot think why the clothes were still so wet,' Mrs Lang was saying as they entered. 'It's almost as if they had been rinsed again.'

Emily shot a suspicious glance at Daniel, who looked sheepish.

'No matter, shall return, for lunch,' responded Fox.

'Fox will be returning tomorrow, his clothes are not dry yet,' Mrs Lang announced as she and Fox entered the room.

Emily tried hard not to smile. 'Oh Fox, seeing that you will have to return, Daniel had something to ask you,' she said.

'Yes, yes, of course,' said Daniel at once. 'Ah,

Emily wanted to ask you to church with us. But she didn't want to embarrass you, in case you, um, don't go to church. I thought I'd ask, er, in case you did. I mean, if you don't go, then just forget I asked.'

Emily bristled at Daniel's little betrayal, but she said nothing. Once again, Daniel looked sheepish.

'Chapel, yours, will attend,' said Fox. 'For invitation, thanks.'

Soon after that Fox was gone, hurrying away to catch the last train. Later, lying in her bed, Emily thought over the day's events, and of what she had learned about Fox. Her father was always saying that modern sailors were too soft, and that the flogging should be brought back as shipboard discipline. Brought *back*. On Fox's ship flogging was still practised. Fox *had* been flogged. Perhaps they still do that sort of thing on Norwegian ships, she decided.

Fox's accent was really odd, too. It was curiously cold, hard and precise, and everything that he said was always perfectly clear. It was almost like some dialect of English, she thought. Fox also knew a way to bring drowned people back to life. Some person in the crowd on the river bank had said that it was a Chinese trick. Perhaps Fox's ship had visited China. Perhaps the strange cinema device from Fox's trousers also came from China. Perhaps the fighting in which BC had died had been in China ... yet the soldiers who had shot BC did not look like Mr Wu at the laundry shop. Emily's thoughts returned to BC, and for a time she again fantasised that he was not dead and that she was nursing him back to health.

Emily sat up in bed, trying to regain control of her mind. Whenever she thought of her rescuer, she was as suspicious as Sherlock Holmes investigating a murder, but when it came to the dead BC, her heart began to hammer and she felt feverish. BC had done nothing for her. BC had died before they had even met. Fox had saved Emily's life, on the other hand, so why could she not worship him? Emily visualised Fox's face. Somehow his neat hair and sad, serious eyes did not spark any sort of romantic feelings in her. BC was a leader, Fox was not. Being a leader was what made BC so special, she decided. Emily knew that she was a good leader, too, but she had nobody to lead. Every time she told Daniel to do something sensible, he did the opposite unless she forced him to do otherwise.

'You're being just like the silly girls at school,' Emily whispered to herself. 'Especially the artistic ones with put-on French accents like Muriel Baker. They lose their hearts to boys from the grammar school just because they dance well, or are sporting heroes. Stop it! Girls like you don't do that.'

It was a hopeless fight. For the first time in her short life, Emily had toppled, and was now falling out of control.

'Well at least I am losing my heart to a brave, handsome, young man, not some stupid schoolboy,'

Emily muttered to herself presently. 'Why, oh why, does he have to be dead?'

At last Emily gave up the battle with the obsession, turned up the wick of her bedside lamp, and gazed at her collection of dolls and bears. Much to her mother's distress, more than half the dolls were of sailors, soldiers, or knights in cardboard armour. Emily did not like dolls, but her mother insisted on giving them to her, so she fought back by dressing them in ways that would annoy her mother. Taking a purple scarf, Emily began cutting out the pattern for a pair of trousers and a coat. Within half an hour one of the dolls was dressed in a hastily stitched purple uniform, and with a scar inked onto its forehead. Emily bandaged its stomach, giving the implication that BC was wounded, not dead.

Finally, with bandaged doll placed at the centre of her collection, Emily blew out the lamp and drifted into sleep.

2

VICTIM

Daniel was out of bed long before his parents the following morning. To his dismay, however, Emily was dressed and having breakfast when he reached the kitchen.

'You're up early,' he said suspiciously as he cut a slice of bread for himself.

'I am always up before you,' she replied. 'You just get up so late that you never know when I am up.'

Daniel said no more. His sister always won all the arguments. If a question had five possible answers, he was sure that she would have all five ready. Nothing he could say ever caught her off guard. His only defence was to have friends that she did not like, otherwise she would quickly introduce herself, prove that she was more interesting than he was, then make them her friends instead. He did his best to annoy her, but even that seemed to go wrong all too often. He had stood up in the boat only because he knew she would be annoyed. She had certainly been annoyed, yet his triumph had lasted only about five seconds.

As he sat munching his toast, Daniel thought about trying to visit someone for a while, someone that Emily disliked, so that she would not go with him. On the other hand, Fox had said he would return before the church service. The service was at eleven, but Fox had not said just how early he would arrive. Visiting a friend might mean he would be away when Fox returned, and for Daniel that was unthinkable. He was determined not to lose Fox to Emily. Suddenly Emily stood up.

'I am going to check on the state of Fox's clothes,' she announced.

Daniel said nothing, but a moment later he realised that she was going to claim the credit for getting Fox's clothes clean. He hurried after her.

'You never worry about clothes, except if they're for your stupid dolls and bears,' said Daniel as he caught up with his sister. 'Why are you interested now?'

'Everything must be perfect for Fox, because he saved us after your stupid antics in the boat! I'll not have you splashing water over his uniform again.'

'How did ...' began Daniel before he caught himself.

'Daniel Lang, I can read you like a very simple book for very young children,' replied Emily.

As usual, Daniel decided to say nothing. He had never yet won an exchange with his older sister. They were taking Fox's violet uniform out of the drying closet when the maid arrived with a basket of washing.

'Oh Miss Emily, I'se so glad ter see yer!' she hissed urgently, ignoring Daniel.

Daniel felt vaguely annoyed. Everyone always went to Emily first.

'What is it, Martha?' asked Emily as she draped Fox's coat over her arm.

'That coat. It ain't nattyrel.'

'What do you mean?'

'There's a stray thread on the left sleeve. I tried to cut it orf, like to be neat, an' … an' it broke me scissors! It's like a bit o' balin' wire.'

'This one?' asked Emily, twirling the strand of thread in her fingers. 'Oh come now, Martha, it is as soft as a kitten's fur.'

'That's not the 'arf of it,' continued Martha. 'Give it 'ere, an' lookey.'

Martha led them outside, and around behind the laundry. The woodpile was located here, along with a chopping block and axe. Martha was what their mother described as a robust girl in rude health; that is to say, she was broad-shouldered and probably the equal of most men in physical strength. She dusted the splinters from the chopping block with the hem of her skirt, then folded Fox's coat and put it there. Next she picked up the axe.

'Martha, what do you think you are doing?' cried Emily. 'Martha, stop!'

But Martha did not stop. She brought the axe around in one mighty, full-bodied swing and chopped down squarely on the folded coat. The axe bounced off. Emily dashed forward at once and snatched the coat away. Daniel stood watching silently.

'Martha, you evil woman!' cried Emily. 'What do you think you're doing, ruining poor Fox's only ...'

Emily's voice trailed away as she held up the coat. There was not the slightest sign of damage on it. Daniel was astounded, and realised that he was standing and staring with his mouth open. He closed his mouth, and hoped that nobody had been watching him.

'Maybe the axe is blunt,' he suggested.

Martha now put a folded sack on the block and picked up the axe. This time the axe head chopped right through the fabric and buried itself in the wood.

'Like I says, ain't nattyrel,' she concluded.

Emily carried Fox's clothes back to the house in silence, and Daniel noticed that she was even frowning a little. That was good, Daniel concluded. It seemed as if Fox might turn out to be one of those people that Emily did not approve of. Were that the case, he just might become friends with Daniel.

'There is something about Fox that does not add up,' said Emily as she began folding the clothes and putting them on the parlour table.

'What have you got against him?' demanded Daniel. 'He saved us, and he's polite and respectable.'

'But his coat! Martha's axe did not even leave a mark on it.'

'So? It could be like chain mail. A sort of cloth that's armour too. I bet it can stop swords and bullets.'

'But chain mail is made of iron rings.'

'So? Ships used to be made of wood, but now they're made of iron.'

Emily held up the coat and looked at it closely. 'I do not see any rings.'

'They might be visible under a microscope.'

'Well, don't just stand there. Get your microscope.'

'No!'

'What?' exclaimed Emily. 'Why not?'

'Because you're trying to spy on him, even though he saved us.'

'Oh, Danny, I'm just curious.'

'Well I think it's only some sort of armour, like chain mail.'

'Why make armour that feels like ordinary cloth?'

'That's so Fox can be protected at all times, like if a mutinous sailor tried to shoot him,' replied Daniel, with a feeling of authority that came from reading more adventure novels than Emily.

For the first time since he could remember, Emily had no answer. I beat her in an argument! thought Daniel. Must write that in my diary.

'There he is now,' said Emily, looking past Daniel through the window to the front gate. 'You must ask him about the coat ...'

'I'll do no such thing!' retorted Daniel. 'If you want to play Sherlock Holmes questioning a criminal, do it yourself. Anyway, you forgot his boots, and I'm going back to the laundry to fetch them.'

To Daniel's relief, Emily did not follow as he marched back out to the laundry. Fox's boots were dry, and the groom had cleaned them. He examined them closely, and concluded that they were probably not made of leather. Just as well Emily didn't notice, he thought as he returned to the house. Emily was waiting at the back door.

'I told Fox that he could change in your room,' she announced. 'I did not think you would mind.'

Daniel said nothing. Emily tried to take the boots, but Daniel snatched them back and pushed past her. Even when she knows I would agree, she does something to make me argue, he thought. Maybe that's why she always wins.

They trod the carpeted stairs softly and slowly. Above them, they could hear Fox singing softly, yet his voice was suddenly like that of the old cockney carter who delivered the firewood. The song was familiar, too.

'He sings like he's English,' whispered Emily.

Slowly and silently, they approached the open door of Daniel's room. Odd, thought Daniel. Fox did not close the door to change his clothes. Fox had his back to them as he stood buttoning his shirt and singing.

> When will you pay me,
> Say the bells of Old Bailey?
> When I grow rich,
> Say the bells of Shoreditch.
> Pray when will that be,
> Say the bells …

Daniel and Emily had made no sound, yet Fox whirled around and flung a small knife. It thudded into the door frame beside Daniel's left ear. Daniel shrank back with a gasp of fright, dropping the boots. Emily darted behind him.

'Daniel!' exclaimed Fox, hurriedly snapping to attention, then bowing. 'Emily, also. Apologies.'

'I … I'm sorry, I startled you,' was all that Daniel could think to say.

Fox strode forward and retrieved his knife from the door frame.

'Fault, is mine,' he said. 'Rustle of cloth, I heard. Of Death's robes, is sound, some places.'

'Oh,' gasped Emily, her voice still unsteady. 'And where might those places be?'

'Long ago, far away.'

'You have been to such horrible, rough places,

yet you are so polite,' said Emily, her voice suddenly sympathetic. 'I thought that sort of thing made people rough.'

'Not everyone. For damage, from knife, to woodwork, apologies.'

'Oh, don't worry, I'll say it was me, playing soldiers,' Daniel volunteered, suddenly feeling proud that he could do something to take the side of Fox.

'Fox, do you know what I find strange about you?' Emily asked. 'You are so very English, yet so strangely foreign, too.'

Daniel cringed. His sister was being friendly, but asking awkward questions. Perhaps if I say nothing Fox will not think I'm on her side, thought Daniel. Why can't I just shout at her not to be so nosy? Am I a coward? Compliment people in a friendly tone and they will soon give up their deepest secrets, his mother had often told them. To Daniel, it seemed a mean thing to do, but Emily did it all the time.

'Is compliment?' asked Fox after one of his strange, blanked-out pauses.

'Yes, it is!' snapped Daniel, finally gathering the courage to challenge his sister. 'It is a compliment, isn't it Emily? You're not trying to make Fox admit he's a criminal or something?'

'Daniel Lang, how dare you be so rude to our guest!' said Emily. 'And after he saved us, too.'

The accusation took Daniel completely by surprise. From being Fox's defender, Daniel now seemed as if he had attacked Fox. Daniel stood in silence, floundering for words. That turned out to be a mistake as well. Emily picked up the boots.

'Here are your boots, Fox, all clean and polished,' she said. 'Is your uniform all right?'

'Smell, is strange.'

'Martha put essence of lavender in the drying closet to make the cloth smell like it's something girls wear,' said Daniel sullenly. 'She does it to my clothes, too.'

'My thanks.'

'And the groom cleaned and polished your boots,' added Emily.

'Again, my thanks,' replied Fox.

Daniel left the room shaking his head, wondering how his sister had suddenly taken charge of the situation so completely. More of those feminine wiles that people keep talking about, he decided. He resolved to make a study of feminine wiles, and wondered if his father had a book about them in his library.

As the Lang family walked along Bay Street with Fox, they met with Mr Aitkinson, the grocer. Daniel found himself stuck with Mr Aitkinson and his father. After refusing to invite Fox to church, then spying on him, Emily was now monopolising him.

'A hero, then?' asked Mr Aitkinson after Mr Lang raised the subject of a job for Fox. 'Well, that's good, but can he keep his mind on the job? You know, deliver packages without a fuss, not stop to talk with idlers on street corners, that sort of thing.'

'He has worked on a ship, Mr Aitkinson, I'm sure he is very reliable and disciplined,' replied Mr Lang.

'Sailors are notorious for thievery.'

'Anything that he steals, I shall replace the worth out of my own pocket.'

'Will you? Well, in that case, I could give him a try. What say tomorrow, then?'

By the time they reached the church Fox had a job, but all through the service Daniel felt uneasy. Mr Aitkinson was not very respectable, even though he was careful not to show it in front of most people. Daniel knew that boys from the neighbourhood who had the right passwords could buy French postcards from the grocer. These featured girls in artistic poses wearing no clothes. Would Fox be corrupted by working for the grocer? If his parents found out, would they forbid him to see Fox? On the other hand, Daniel had managed to acquire a few of Mr Aitkinson's postcards from one of his own contacts, yet he did not feel corrupt.

By the closing hymn Daniel had concluded that if Fox's moral standards had survived life aboard a ship, then Mr Aitkinson was unlikely to damage them. Suddenly Daniel realised that Fox had known all the right responses, prayers and hymns throughout the service. Daniel thought back to the song that

Fox had been singing when he and Emily had surprised him. Fox spoke with a heavy accent, yet he sang like an Englishman.

Fox was predictably polite and well-mannered during Sunday lunch, almost to the point of being boring. After the meal, he and Daniel played chess and Fox won six games in a row. That's my problem, thought Daniel. I never think ahead. Mr Lang proposed a challenge match. Again Fox won. Fox was playing Emily when Daniel decided to go to the kitchen for a drink. It was now that Martha approached him.

'I didn't want to alarm the old folks, Master Daniel, so I come to you,' the maid explained. 'It's that Fox again.'

Daniel knew that for Martha to talk to him about anything at all was very unusual.

'What's he done?' he asked, his heart sinking.

'There's things missin'. Odd things from the medicine cabinet, pantry and laundry. Some little empty jars are gone from the wood yard pile, an' I swear there's some bicarb of soda, Condy's crystals, bleach, lemons, and suchlike gone from the bottles and packets. It was probably taken last night, like.'

Daniel thought about this for some moments. One of his own friends, the notorious Barry the Bag, was liable to steal nearly anything that was not nailed down, but he would draw the line at Condy's crystals, bleach, and empty jars. He was more likely to

steal a bottle of wine than lemons. Daniel was sure
that this was something to do with Fox.

'It must have been one of my friends,' Daniel
decided. 'I'll get him to pay us back.'

'I didn't think any'd come round since Friday.'

'If Barry the Bag was going to steal something,
he would have kept out of your sight,' said Daniel
firmly.

'But I'm sure the little rat hasn't been 'ere since
Friday.'

'He might have,' countered Daniel.

This had more than the desired effect on Martha,
who lost colour and clasped her hands anxiously. Mr
Lang had ordered her to keep an eye on Daniel's
friends after the last bottle of wine had gone missing.
If she had missed a visit from Barry the Bag, it would
not go well with her.

'Er, d'yer think Mr Lang will take it out o' me
wages, like?' Martha asked.

'No, and I shall put in a good word for you if he
asks,' Daniel assured her.

'Oh young sir, would yer really? I been 'aving a
bad time of it lately, an' I'd hate ter add another blot
ter me copybook.'

'I'm not Emily, you don't have to worry,' said
Daniel. 'Now, um, can you do something else for
me?'

'Oh aye, anything.'

'Promise to say nothing about this to anyone but me.'

'Oh aye, that I will.'

'And if anything else is stolen, let me know at once.'

'That I will, young master, betcha life on it.'

Daniel dashed out of the house and ran to the local railway station to speak with Barry the Bag. Barry was about Daniel's age, and issued and collected tickets at the station when his father was too drunk to be on duty. As far as Daniel could tell, this was most of the time. Barry was extracting tobacco from discarded cigarettes for resale to his father's friends when Daniel arrived.

'Dan the Man, man o' mine!' called the short, thin and very shifty-looking Barry as Daniel arrived.

Mrs Lang said that Barry always looked as if he were about to snatch something and run. In fact Barry never snatched anything. He just had a way of picking up things as if they were his, then walking away with them. Barry held out a tobacco-stained hand to Daniel. Barry was the only person that Daniel knew who had tobacco stains on his fingers but did not smoke.

'Look, Barry, I don't have much time,' began Daniel.

'That's the way it is, Dan Man. Them wot has it all don't have no time, them wot's resourcefully deprived like me got all the time in the world.'

'Last night, do you remember selling a ticket to someone about my height and dressed like me?'

'Yeah, now that you mention it. Cove with real neat hair, talked like a foreigner.'

'Yes, yes. Barry, tell me all about him. Did he do anything odd?'

'Dunno, nothin' much to tell. The bloke stood about on the platform, then got on the train. Oh, an' he checked some stuff from 'is pockets. Little jars, lemons, that's all I could see. Wasn't really lookin' if the truth be known.'

'Things are missing back at the house …'

Barry suddenly went on the defensive; that is, he cringed slightly then glanced to his right and left.

'I only polished off the scotch wot was left in yer old man's glass!' he protested softly. 'You know, like the Bible says. Waste not, want not.'

'The Bible doesn't say that.'

'Doesn't it? So, wot's gone?'

'Condy's crystals.'

'Wot's that?'

'Potassium permanganate. It turns water purple.'

'Shit, eh? Wot else?'

'Bleach.'

'Yeah, I've heard o' that. Wot is it?'

'It turns white cloth white.'

'Turns white things white? Ain't that one o' those astrologies ya told me about, like when ya say the same thing twice when ya only need to say it once?'

'I think you mean tautologies.'

'Yeah.'

'What about missing jars?'

'Jars of wot?'

'Empty jars.'

Barry burst out laughing.

'Dan the Man, ya been at yer old man's scotch or wot? Me, take jars full of bleach and, er, that other stuff? Ya want my opinion?'

'That's why I'm here, Barry!' muttered Daniel impatiently.

'I reckon ya got a visitor wot's a dodgy leaf, and who's doin' laundry, an' I reckon it's that cove wot bought the tikky last night.'

Daniel thought about this for some moments.

'As much as I hate to admit it, Barry, I fear you are right.'

Daniel returned home to find Mrs Lang playing the piano while Mr Lang sang some song about being a modern major general. Fox, Emily and Martha were their audience. Daniel was very uneasy about the situation. On the one hand, he owed Fox his life, yet what did one do if one owed one's life to a thief? Emily seemed to think that she always had an answer for everything. Daniel hated to admit it, but she did seem to have been right about Fox. Fox had to be followed, but there was a problem with that. Daniel had no money for the train. Emily had money, however. She never did anything wrong, so her allowance was never stopped. Far from hiding the thefts from her, Daniel decided that he would confront her with them. Daniel beckoned to Emily from the parlour doorway. She seemed quite anxious to leave the room, which was understandable, given their father's singing voice.

'It was so humiliating. I beat Fox at chess!' she exclaimed softly as they reached the kitchen. 'I could see that he was trying, too. What will he think of me? Mother will never let me hear the end of it.'

'Listen!' hissed Daniel. 'Please, just listen. Things have been stolen.'

'What things?' demanded Emily at once. 'If that Barry has …'

'Shush! Keep your voice down.'

'Well, what things?'

'Small, odd things. Empty jars, Condy's crystals, bleach, lemons.'

'It *must* have been that horrid Barry the Bag from the railway station.'

'He said he didn't.'

'And you believed him? That dirty little ruffian who sells those, those, er, horrid French pictures of women doing shameful things.'

'They're art pictures, and besides, he says he only delivers them for Mr Aitkinson.'

'They're pictures of orgies!' insisted Emily.

'You don't even know what orgies are!'

'Yes I do!'

'Well, what are they?'

'They're dinner parties that respectable people don't go to.'

'How would you know?' Daniel demanded. 'Have you ever seen one?'

'I don't have to. From all the filthy giggles and whispers that I have overheard from you and your ruffian friends, I *know* what they must be like, and –'

'All right, all right, Emmy, look, what about Fox? Martha noticed things missing last night.'

'Martha? Why didn't she tell me?'

'I asked her not to, I wanted to check with Barry first.'

'Barry would never admit to stealing anything.'

'Would Barry steal bleach and lemons?'

'Perhaps not,' Emily conceded.

'Barry says that Fox bought a ticket for Flinders Street, and that while he was waiting for the train he took jars and lemons from his pockets and looked at them. He told me this before I said that anything had been stolen.'

'Well then, Fox was quite probably building something scientific, something to do with electricity. He's very clever.'

She's changed! thought Daniel. The moment I change sides, she changes the other way. She must do it to annoy me, and for no other reason. Daniel was surprised that he had never noticed this before.

'Well that's all right, then,' concluded Daniel, who then turned and began to walk away.

'Wait!' called Emily. 'You have to tell someone.'

'Why? You approve of what he did.'

'I never said that –' began Emily.

'Then tell Father.'

For some moments, Emily squirmed. Daniel stood watching, in no mood to give her any way out.

'It *is* odd,' admitted Emily finally. 'I mean, Mother would have given him whatever he wanted willingly, if he had asked.'

'She would also have asked why he wanted it. Mother is very nosy. What if he didn't want anyone to know?'

This seemed enough to convince Emily that the matter was to be taken seriously. She thought carefully, her arms tightly folded across her chest.

'Danny, Martha said another bottle of wine went missing some days ago.'

'What?' exclaimed Daniel in alarm. 'But I watch Barry very carefully now.'

'Not carefully enough, it seems. What happened to you last time?'

'Three strokes of the cane from Father, and I had to pay for a new bottle out of my allowance.'

'Well then, I have a proposal for you. I shall pay Martha to replace that bottle out of my savings if you will ask Fox about the missing things.'

I had beaten her! he fumed silently. I had her cornered. I won the argument. What did she do? Daniel tried to think logically. She changed the argument, I suppose.

'So, the missing bottle was something you were saving up to win the next argument,' said Daniel.

'Daniel!' shouted Emily, stamping her foot. 'What a despicable thing to say.'

'Explain why it isn't true,' responded Daniel.

Once again Emily squirmed. She liked to win, and he was getting tired of being beaten.

'The bottle is still missing,' she reminded him.

'Then tell Father. I can take another caning.'

It was a high price to pay to slip out of his sister's grip, but Daniel had decided that it was worth it.

'No! Danny, look, we need to do something about Fox. I know he saved us, but if he is a thief, well, who knows what he might take next?'

'I think I should follow him.'

'No!'

'Why not?'

'Because it's better to ask him.'

'No it isn't. If I ask him, he could lie. If I follow him, I'll know for sure.'

Daniel had one important factor in his favour. He was allowed out alone, and Emily was not.

'All right then, do so,' she muttered reluctantly.

'I have no money for the train, and Fox travels by train.'

'No money?' asked Emily. 'Why not? Too many sweets from Mr Aitkinson?'

'Our parents think I can be kept out of trouble by stopping my pocket money every time I even pick my nose, that's why I have no money. Well?'

'Yes, all right, I'll give you money for the fare. How much is it?'

Daniel quoted her a little more than the price of a return ticket to the city. As he had hoped, she did not know the price of a ticket. She hurried upstairs to get the money, leaving Daniel in the kitchen. I did it, I beat her, he thought. He sat down on a chair, almost dizzy with shock and relief. Emily returned with her purse.

'Find out where he goes and what he does,' she said as she counted out the coins.

'And you won't tell Mother and Father?'

'Of course not! Remember what I said? Fox may be innocent. He may be doing some science class at a mechanics institute, to better himself. We may even be able to help him.'

'He would ask if he wanted help.'

'Nonsense. He may be too embarrassed.'

Daniel watched from a distance as Fox bought a ticket at the railway station, then walked up the platform and stood with his cap pulled over his eyes. Now Daniel went to the ticket window.

'Dan the Man, yer back again,' said Barry from behind the window. 'And where would you be goin' this fine Sunday?'

Barry the Bag was still standing in for his father, who was probably asleep in one of the station's rooms.

Daniel thought quickly. 'Same as my friend, Fox,' he heard himself say.

'Flinders Street it is, Danny Boy, except that I expect you want a return tikky. Funny cove, don't know why he didn't get a return tikky when he came out 'ere. Oi, remember that postcard wot I showed you a while back?'

Daniel blushed at once.

'Yes, the, er, artistic photograph of the, er, French girl.'

'Yeah, well, old man Aitkinson's got a new bundle in and he says that they're amazin'ly artistic. I got some old ones, an' I thought, like, you'd like 'em for sixpence. That's tuppence each, a real bargain.'

'You mean three?' asked Daniel, torn between alarm and curiosity.

'Yeah, look, I got 'em 'ere. See, she's takin' 'er bathin' costume off, and 'ere's one sittin' on a swing – that's a good one, she's showin' the lot. And lookey, two sittin' on a barrel. That's two for one card, a penny each at tuppence, you know?'

The whistle of a train sounded in the distance. Daniel glanced about, saw that nobody was watching, tried to convince himself that he had to buy the three postcards so that Barry would not become suspicious, then handed over his sixpence. That left only one other sixpence for emergencies, but then Daniel had got a strange feeling of satisfaction from spending Emily's money on filthy pictures. Moments later he found himself on the platform with three French postcards in his coat pocket. He sat down and raised a newspaper he had taken from the rubbish bin, even though the train was approaching. The train chuffed into the station and stopped. Daniel waited until Fox was making for a carriage before he lowered his paper, got up, and hurried to board the train.

The engine blew its whistle, then chuffed into life. The stations came and went, and people boarded and left the train. Daniel imagined that each and every one of them could see through his jacket to the postcards that were in his pocket. Some German doctor had invented rays that could do just that. He had heard his father talking about it. The German machine could even see through women's clothing.

'Roentgen Rays or something,' he whispered to himself, then wondered if any other passengers might be carrying a machine that could generate them. What was that rhyme about them?

Daniel felt for the three incriminating cards in his pocket. *Why bother with my dirty postcards when there's real women to look at?* Daniel assured himself with a guilty glance about the carriage. Two rather serious-looking men wearing top hats were staring out of the windows, while a strict-looking middle-aged mother sat between two daughters of around sixteen. Both girls were studiously staring at bibles, but neither had turned a page in ten minutes. *Do girls dream about boys who have their clothes off?* Daniel wondered.

It seemed an eternity before they reached the Richmond railway station. By now literally everything was suggesting women to Daniel's tortured imagination.

> Sweet lass of Richmond Hill
> Sweet lass of Richmond Hill
> I'll crown design
> To make you mine
> Sweet lass of Richmond Hill.

The words of the song sounded so loudly in his mind that Daniel was sure the other passengers would hear. None gave any sign of doing so, however. Daniel tried to distract himself by recalling that the original Richmond Hill was in England. The train chugged away from the platform, and soon they were approaching Flinders Street Station.

Daniel waited until he could see Fox on the station platform before he got out of the carriage. He followed the youth out of the station, then watched him walk down Swanston Street and turn into Flinders Lane. That was not a very respectable area, according to what his mother said. Tailors and dressmakers had workshops there, along with artists and loose women. This must be where the photographs for the postcards are taken, Daniel decided, suddenly worried about the dangers of walking down a street crowded with loose French women. To his immense relief, Flinders Lane was deserted. Daniel saw Fox turn into a dilapidated building and vanish from sight. He slunk forward, close to the shuttered shopfronts, trying to seem invisible. A face appeared at a window on the top floor and glanced down at the lane before withdrawing again.

Without warning Daniel was jerked back into an alley by his collar, spun around, tripped, and slammed down into a pile of foul-smelling rags. His arms were twisted up behind his back as he gasped for breath, then his wrists were bound and finally a cloth was stuffed into his mouth. Hands scrabbled through Daniel's pockets, and his postcards were removed.

'Oi, dirty little cove, inne?' laughed someone.

At last the gang was satisfied that his pockets were empty. Daniel felt his arms being untied, but he was not inclined to fight. A foot shoved him out of the alley. He picked himself up and broke into a run, pulling the balled-up rag from his mouth as he made for the bustle of Swanston Street. He checked his pockets, and discovered that nothing at all had been left to him. Not a coin, not a return railway ticket, and certainly not a French postcard. He ran all the way to Flinders Street Station, and did not stop until he was on the platform.

Now Daniel contemplated his options. Home was seven miles away. At a brisk walking pace that was about two hours, and it was already late in the afternoon. Daniel decided that he would take the train, in spite of having no ticket. Barry might be checking the tickets at North Brighton, after all.

'Times are really desperate when Barry the Bag is my only hope,' he muttered as he boarded a train on cramped, unsteady legs.

Daniel was close to throwing up with anxiety as he got off the train at North Brighton, and he made a show of stopping to tie a loose shoelace on the platform. He had in fact untied the lace aboard the train. As he had hoped, he was the last person to approach the ticket collector at the gate. Even better, that collector was Barry the Bag.

'Barry, I haven't got a ticket!' hissed Daniel as he reached the short, ratty youth.

''Course ya have, I sold ya one not three hours back!' laughed Barry.

'You don't understand, I've been robbed!'

'Robbed?' exclaimed Barry, who had endured a very dull day at the station, and was in the mood to be entertained.

'Yes! They took everything. My money, my ticket and the postcards.'

Daniel held out his wrists, which still had the red weals left by whatever had been used to tie them. Barry whistled, even more impressed, then rushed Daniel across the walkway between the platforms and into the ticket office.

'Get this inter the body, Dan,' said Barry, handing him a mug with dark, steaming liquid in it.

'What is it?'

'Coffee, it's mine.'

'Mother says coffee is the drink of the devil!'

'How'd she know? She ever met 'im?'

Just then someone arrived to buy a ticket. While Barry attended the window, Daniel sipped at Barry's mug of coffee. It tasted foul, but it had a curious strength about it, and Daniel was ready to try anything that might restore his strength. Barry returned.

'Now then, man o' mine, ya was rolled by a push?'

'No, I was robbed by ruffians.'

'That's wot I said. And they took the cards?'

'Yes, and I really liked that one of the girl on the swing, too.'

'Cor, so did I. Was all set to buy it back. Ya hurt?'

'Not really. I was taken from behind and pinned down. It was in an alley, I was watching someone.'

'Yeah? Who?'

'A friend. Fox.'

'Spyin' on 'im?'

'Well, yes. No! Er, not quite. More or less.'

There was a long and awkward silence. Presently Barry rubbed his face with both hands, then took Daniel by the shoulders.

'Ya really don't know the streets,' he said.

'Know the streets?'

'Thought as much. Listen, is your mate Fox on the run?'

'No, he was walking.'

'I mean are the coppers onter 'im?'

'Well, that's what I was hoping to find out, but –'

'Ya need to be told a few things, Danny Boy. Important things. Meantime, take this to raise the spirits, like.'

Barry thrust a postcard into Daniel's hand. It featured a rather cheery-looking girl with a fencing foil in her hand, but she was rather immodestly sitting backwards on a chair. This little indiscretion was overwhelmed by the fact that she was wearing no clothes at all, however.

'You're too kind,' mumbled Daniel miserably.

'Nah, we art fanciers gotta stick together.'

Daniel sat sipping at Barry's coffee as his friend and associate sold more tickets for the next train to the city. He took out the postcard that Barry had just given him and stared at it for some time. It was curiously alluring, but he had no idea why.

Barry was the most notoriously wicked boy in the neighbourhood, according to Mrs Lang, yet Barry was the only person who would, or even could, show Daniel any sympathy on this, the worst day of his life. Barry, whose bag was always full of things that were for sale, and had seldom been paid for when their previous owners had parted company with them. Daniel felt absolutely wretched, yet this also made him feel as if he had nothing to lose. If he ever again had to do anything that involved criminals, he was going to make sure Barry was there to look after him.

3

LEADER

Ever since she had seen the image of BC on Saturday night, Emily had not been able to get him out of her mind. BC had been so brave, BC had fought with more courage than Jason, or Horatio, or any boy in an adventure novel. Even when mortally wounded, he was shouting at Three to ... to do what? Destroy a machine. What machine? Some terrible machine built by some terrible enemy. That had to be it. Images of BC cascaded through Emily's mind as she lay there on her bed. BC running, BC leading, BC fighting ... and BC covered in blood, dying.

There was nothing that Emily could do to clear her mind of the images. She got up, took out a pencil and a sheaf of art paper, then tried to sketch BC from memory. Several attempts at a portrait from memory produced no real likeness of BC.

'Well, I'd rather be bad at art than be like Muriel Baker, with her French accent and French beret, and, and French morals,' muttered Emily, who then took the violet uniform off her doll and began sewing the coat more carefully.

As the afternoon passed she remade her doll in a better image of BC, cutting its hair, painting out its rosy cheeks, and giving it a sort of stubby rifle weapon that consisted of several pencils and parts of a matchbox tied together with string. If only Mother knew, Emily thought with grim satisfaction.

When Emily came down for dinner, Mrs Lang remarked that she looked very pale. Emily said that she had a slight headache, and returned to her room as soon as the meal was over. It was not until late that night that Daniel approached Emily to report on his adventure for the day. By then she was already in bed, with the reading lamp burning.

'Fox went all the way to Flinders Street Station,' Daniel reported sheepishly. 'Then he went to a building in Flinders Lane. A lot of tailors seem to have shops there, but they were all closed. It was, er, well, hard to follow him after that.'

'You mean you do not know where he went?'

'I did my best. At least I saw the building he lives in, and what floor he went to.'

'What did you do then?'

'I returned to Flinders Street Station and came back here.'

Emily thought for some moments.

'Tomorrow is Monday. Mr Aitkinson has given Fox a job, so he will not be in his rooming house. I think that we shall search his room in the morning. You have a day off school, and I shall tell Mother that I have a slight chill from being half-drowned on Saturday.'

'Perhaps we could hide behind ... *we*?'

Daniel's eyes were bulging, but more with shock than fear.

'Both of us are going.'

'But you're a girl!'

'And you are a little boy.'

'I'm big for my age, I'm as big as Fox, and —'

'And you did not do everything that I told you today. I shall have to be there, to supervise.'

'But —'

'I think that Fox has done something terrible.'

'What do you mean?'

'Stolen something, and perhaps worse. I saw his ... his journal.'

'What? You mean a book?'

'Well, er, yes, a sort of book. He has been in some sort of fight. Daniel, as much as I am grateful to Fox, I think we might have to tell the police about him.'

'But what did he do?'

'That is what we must find out before we say anything to anyone. He may be innocent. We cannot judge him before we know what he has done.'

Although Emily generally felt trapped by being a girl, she made sure that people always saw her behaving well, and she had a reputation for being clever and diligent. It was true that she often forced her younger brother on illicit missions to fetch adventure and romance novels that were considered unsuitable for young ladies to read, but that was as far as her sense of rebellion ever went.

Now Emily's world had changed, however. She had seen BC die. She had seen him die through Fox's eyes, via some type of very expensive camera that he had been carrying, one of the new cameras that recorded moving pictures. Above all, Emily desperately wanted to make sure that BC did not die in vain. For her, it would be a crime were BC not remembered as a hero. She had no idea what he had done, but he had died a hero's death, so he was obviously a hero.

Emily resembled her mother more than she liked to admit, because both were very forceful, and not afraid of confronting people. They were both pillars of the British Empire, the solid foundations that their menfolk built upon. Emily wanted to be the pillar on which the monument to BC would rest, but unless she could learn about him, there could be no monument. Fox was the key to everything, he actually knew BC, and his image machine preserved BC's last moments. Emily decided that she would soon face Fox with all the things that she had learned. She would threaten to go to the police, and that would make him tell her everything about BC and his death. What had he been like? she wondered. True heroes have sweethearts at home who are frail and beautiful, so any girl who could take BC's fancy would be exquisite indeed. Had there been such a girl?

'Probably tiny and delicate, with golden curls, like that sniffling little Cecily Thomson,' muttered Emily, glaring at a class photograph on her wall. 'Or would a hero love someone big, bold and healthy like Juliet Bristow? Could someone evil and artistic like Muriel Baker ensnare his heart?'

As usual, Emily thought things through logically. She did not have to be such a girl. She was going to have to be a soldier for BC instead, because Daniel had proved himself to be unreliable. Soldiers did things to make themselves fitter and stronger. Emily knew that. Removing her shoes, she ran up and down the stairs several dozen times. That seemed to transform her thighs and calves into a pair of large pincushions filled with red-hot needles and razors. On her father's theory that anything uncomfortable must be good for you, she allowed herself to enjoy a sense of triumph. She was training to defend BC's memory. People would know her as BC's champion, even though BC was gone forever.

The matter of a weapon was somewhat harder. There was, of course, her father's collection of guns, but she knew nothing about using them, and was frightened of guns. There were sharp knives in the kitchen, but the idea of going into battle with a kitchen knife seemed too silly for words. Thus it was that Emily borrowed a letter opener in the shape of a sword from her father's study. It was only nine inches long, and did not have enough of an edge to even sharpen a pencil, but at least it looked the part and the point was quite sharp. Emily had seen Daniel at fencing practice, so she had some idea of how one held a sword.

The following morning Emily nearly abandoned her expedition several times through sheer embarrassment, but each time the feeling washed over her she fought back. There was the matter of missing school, but she feigned a sore throat because of her dunking in the river, and that was enough to convince her mother. With her father gone to his business, and her mother away at some charity meeting at the vicarage, Emily briefed Martha with a covering story, then left with Daniel for the railway station.

Once they were actually on the platform, Emily relaxed. It was too late to abandon the adventure. They were going into a sort of battle and, like BC she was in charge of a squad doing something dangerous. Admittedly she commanded only Daniel, and was armed with a letter opener, but for Emily even that was quite bold. The thought of what BC might think of a girl who was forceful enough to get mixed up in her own adventures was worrying, but that was not an issue she would ever have to face.

It was while Emily sat on a station bench,

contemplating BC and what she could remember
of his face, that Daniel arrived with Barry the Bag.
Barry looked very unhappy.

'He goes with us, or I do not!' said Daniel firmly
before Emily could speak, then he turned back to
Barry. 'Barry, you know Aitkinson's Groceries?'

''Course I do, I buy me postcards from there …
oh, and the groceries, for me old man.'

'Fox is working there this morning.'

'If 'e manages to lift a few postcards, tell 'im I can
move 'em along for sixpence per –'

'Do you always *buy* your postcards?' asked
Daniel.

'Ya mean does I ever pinch any?'

'Yes.'

'Can't. Old Aitkinson keeps 'em locked in a drawer.
Take me a minute to pick that lock, and he's never
gone for that long.'

'So, you can pick locks.'

'Well yeah, I suppose.'

'Barry, I'm not very good at being dishonest.'

'That's a factual.'

'Could *you* … pick a lock for me?'

'Wot? Git aht!'

'I mean it.'

'From Aitkinson?'

'No, from Fox. He lives in Flinders Lane, and –'

'Daniel!' exclaimed Emily. 'You can't do that!
Picking locks is dishonest.'

'Well, how else do we get into his room?'

'We shall ask the lady at the reception desk for a key.'

'The place had **CONDEMNED** written on the door,' said Daniel. 'Do you really think they have a reception desk?'

'I hates to be in agreement with yer sister, Danny Boy, but —'

'Stay out of this!' cried Daniel. 'Emmy, we are about to do something criminal, so we need a criminal to help us.'

'Now just a minute,' began Barry.

'Shut up!' snapped Daniel. 'Well, Emmy?'

'I suppose so,' said Emily reluctantly.

'I never said I'd help!' protested Barry.

'About the canings I got when you stole those bottles of wine?'

'I'll help, I s'pose. But look, just so I knows when we all gets thrown in the slammer, just wot are we doin' and why?' asked Barry.

'I just want to know what Fox is up to,' said Emily. 'I mean, I know he saved me, but we can't let a criminal visit our house.'

'Ya have *me* over,' Barry pointed out.

'Daniel has you over, not me. Besides, Fox may be a bigger criminal than you.'

'Just about everyone's bigger than me. Well, okay. Wot ya want done?'

'Can you pick locks quickly?'

'Yeah, can I ever!'

'Good. Pick the lock to Fox's room, and we shall go in and look around. If we find nothing suspicious, we shall just leave as if we never went near the place.'

They sat together in embarrassed silence until the train arrived, then boarded and found seats away from the other passengers.

'This is daft, and probably dangerous too,' muttered Daniel as the steam train rattled and chugged its way to the city.

'It is nothing of the sort!' insisted Emily. 'We shall just go to the building and find out things.'

'What things?'

'Important things.'

'What if there's nothing to find out? What if Fox returns while we are there?'

'Well then, we shall leap out and demand that he explain everything.'

'But what if he has a gun?'

'He will not shoot us.'

'How do you know?'

'He saved our lives, silly. Someone who saves your life will be too noble to shoot you.'

'He didn't save *my* life!' exclaimed Barry nervously.

'Well, you can stay hiding while I step out and surprise him,' declared Emily.

'If there's somewhere to hide,' said Daniel.

'It's easy to hide,' said Emily.

'How would a girl know that?' demanded Daniel. 'Have you ever tried to hide?'

'Of course. I have hidden under the table in the parlour and listened to Mother and Father talk about all sorts of things.'

'Such as what?' asked Daniel.

'Well … I heard them say that Henry the groom reduced Martha the maid.'

'Reduced her?' responded Daniel. 'You mean made her smaller?'

'How am I to know? Anyway, Father was all for sending her away for being a loose woman.'

'You mean she did naked poses, like in Barry's postcards?'

'We two gotta have a serious talk 'bout some embarrassin' stuff if we live through the next couple of hours, Danny Boy,' muttered Barry, wiping his forehead with a grubby handkerchief.

'Martha would never do a thing like that,' insisted Emily, ignoring Barry. 'Anyway, Mother said good maids are too hard to find, so Father agreed to give her another chance.'

'Reduced. Do you know what that means, Barry?'

'I think he said seduced,' said Barry unhappily.

'What does it mean?'

'Somethin' rude.'

'If it is anything to do with those French postcards, you would be sure to know!' snorted Emily. 'I don't want to hear any more on the subject.'

Barry literally sagged with relief. Judging from his reaction, Emily decided that either she or her brother had just managed to make complete fools of themselves. She resolved to look up the word 'seduced' next time she was within reach of a dictionary.

At Flinders Street Station they left the train, and Daniel led the way to a four-storey building in Flinders Lane that was all peeling paint and rotting woodwork. The outer door was closed, but it yielded to Barry's picklock.

They ascended the stairs to the top floor, exploring as they went. All the rooms on the first three floors were empty and open, and Emily began to suspect that her brother had made a mistake. They communicated by gestures, even though the floorboards creaked louder than a whisper with every step they took. There was a pile of crates on the landing of the top floor, and nearby was a door that was closed. Barry pointed at it and whispered, 'That'll be it.'

Just as he spoke they heard the outer door creak open far below, then came footsteps on the stairs. They slipped behind the empty wooden crates and huddled down out of sight. The newcomer's footsteps continued on the stairs, and it was soon clear that he was going to come all the way to the top. He had the same brisk, military step that Emily had become used to hearing when Fox was on the stairs at home.

Emily heard a rapid but oddly purposeful series of taps on the door. A half dozen taps replied from within, then the visitor responded with several more. There is another person in the room, she concluded, blind panic suddenly paralysing her limbs. Fox seems noble, but he might have associations with criminals who are not. The door creaked open.

'Reporting …' began Fox's voice.

'Sensor, scoping, intruders!' barked a voice that should not have existed. 'Three, bearing, zero zero. Profile, concealed. Armament, knife, one. Status, crouching!'

Emily felt light-headed and on the verge of fainting as the seconds ticked by. Both she and Daniel had made the floorboards creak as they had walked across the landing to hide behind the crates, but the person who glided into view and loomed over them had somehow made no sound at all.

Emily recognised one of the stubby fire-rifles from the scene in Fox's image machine. She was now seeing it from the most disturbing angle possible, however. The person holding it wore black trousers, a strip of white bandage around his stomach, and had a blue shirt caked with dried blood under an unbuttoned military jacket. His face was familiar; in fact, his face had been etched indelibly into Emily's memory two days earlier.

Fox stepped into view. The instant that he saw

Emily and Daniel he sighed, then raised his eyes to the ceiling.

'BC, threat status, zero,' Fox explained to the youth.

'Identify,' ordered the bandaged BC.

'Emily, Daniel, railway official,' he said, then turned to the crouching, terrified trio. 'Knife?' he said as he held out his hand.

They stood up slowly, holding their hands high, then Emily surrendered her letter opener. With a flicker of an expression that might have been contempt, BC thumbed something on his weapon, then gestured to the open door and said, 'In.'

At first glance there was only rubbish in the room, but BC had a bed of blankets and newspapers set up behind some boxes in a corner, so that any watchman casually checking the room would see nothing suspicious. Beside the bed were several bottles of water, some fruit and sausage, and other small, bright things that Emily did not recognise at all. An open window looked out onto a gutter between two roofs. The word toilet floated through Emily's mind. After all, Daniel had once been in the habit of peeing through his bedroom window into the guttering because he was too lazy to go downstairs to the toilet – at least until the vicar, the deacon,

and half a dozen members of the Ladies' Auxiliary
Council of the parish had observed him in the act
from their tea party next door. That had ended his
pocket money for so long that he had had to ferry
suspicious packages for Barry the Bag on his bicycle
to earn his own money.

'Sit,' ordered BC, closing the door and pointing
to a corner.

Emily, Daniel and Barry sat on the floor, their
arms still raised. Suddenly BC seemed to weaken,
then sway. He sat down hastily on one of the boxes.
For the first time Emily realised how very small BC
was; in fact, he was shorter than Daniel. He was of a
curiously slight, almost frail build, yet his eyes blazed
with authority.

'Railway official, state name,' said BC in a tone
that demanded an honest answer on pain of death.

'Barry. Barry the Bag, er, like, Barry Porter, that is.
I'm a mate of Dan the Man.'

'That's me,' explained Daniel.

'BC, status?' asked Fox with concern that bor-
dered on alarm.

'Benzothoractine, myself, for use of, depleted,'
replied BC. 'Pain, severe.'

'Why's the young cove called BC?' whispered
Barry to Daniel.

'Battle Commander,' said BC, who had somehow heard the whisper from right across the room.
'Parade name, Liore-BC. Battle standard name, BC.

British Imperial SYS-IK Cadets.'

Truly exceptional hearing, thought Emily. Now she noticed that a spot of blood had appeared on the bandage at the centre of BC's stomach.

'Excuse me Master BC, but you seem unwell, and um ...' Emily's voice trailed away as her mind finally caught up with her tongue and pointed out just how utterly ridiculous her words were probably sounding.

BC looked to Emily, then to Fox. 'Joking, is?' asked BC wearily.

'Sixteen,' explained Fox. 'Young, naive.'

'Sixteen?' exclaimed BC, casting a suspicious glance back at Emily before pointing to himself. 'Three, explain, more. Am fifteen, am Battle Commander. After twelve, naive, nobody is.'

More was said in the ensuing minutes, but Emily's mind had gone blank through absolute and complete mortification. BC, the youth who had been her obsession over the two days past, was alive. Emily should have been overjoyed about this, yet she could not recall ever being so unhappy. BC, her idol, her god, had caught her armed with a letter opener, wearing a pink dress with white ruffle frills, and cowering behind a packing case between her younger brother and Barry the Bag. Worst of all, the deadly, courageous, dynamic BC now knew Emily's age ... and Emily was a year older than BC.

Mrs Lang had always said that people should do what they did best, and not try to be what they were not. For all of Emily's mortification, one thing was all too clear to her, and that was BC's condition. He was sick, injured, and in pain. Further, he was certainly not being looked after properly. Blood was seeping through his bandages, and quite possibly the wound was infected. He had no proper bed, and his food did not look at all nourishing. Worst of all, there was nobody to care for him. Attempting to gather some dignity together, Emily took a deep breath and opened her mouth. Fox and BC immediately focussed on her. Emily lost her nerve for a moment, exhaled with her mouth still open, then took another breath.

'BC, you need to be looked after properly,' Emily managed.

'Am soldier,' said BC, as if this explained everything.

'Even soldiers need to be looked after.'

'Fox, medi-tech,' declared BC.

'Er, Fox is too young to be a doctor,' guessed Emily.

'Medi-tech!' insisted BC, gesturing to Fox with a bloody hand before clutching at his stomach again.

'You need someone with you all the time. You need to come home with us.'

'Home?' asked BC, turning to Fox. 'Define?'

'Small courtly-house,' explained Fox.

This answer did not appear to satisfy BC, but events suddenly overtook the youth. His eyes lost focus, the gun fell from his hand, and he began to topple. Fox caught him and laid him out on the bedding on the floor. His manner was efficient and brisk, rather than caring and gentle. Emily began to get up, but Fox turned on her.

'Back!' he said in a soft but urgent voice. 'BC, my charge.'

'He'll die if he's not nursed properly.'

'Soldiers die,' responded Fox, looking down at BC with what might have been sadness.

'But he doesn't have to die!'

'Battle status!' insisted Fox.

'This is not a battlefield!' retorted Emily.

'Battlefield, is!' snapped Fox. 'World, all, battlefield is. BC dies. Am left. Will fight. Sometime, will die.'

'I reckon the cove with the gun wins the argument,' said Barry, who had spent his life trying to convince people who were bigger and stronger than he was that they should not bother hitting him.

'If BC is dying, than it should not matter what happens to him!' declared Emily defiantly.

While Fox's battle language was very effective for quick, clear communications in desperate, deadly situations, it was not particularly effective for arguments.

'I...' began Fox, then he stopped. 'BC, must protect,'

he finally managed. 'Battle Commander, clearthink.'

'I want to protect him too!' declared Emily. 'We must get him home.'

'No! Dangerous!'

'Why is home, where he can be cared for, more dangerous than here, where, well, anyone may walk in while he lies in a faint?'

The truly good thing about arguing with Fox was that he argued strictly by logic. Defeat his logic, and he was convinced. He stood in silence, then thumped his fist to his chest in some sort of salute.

'Suggestions?' he asked.

Emily caught sight of some familiar-looking items from home. Among them were jars, bandages, ointments, and even needles, tweezers, a scalpel and waxed threads.

'You have been trying to treat BC's wound,' observed Emily.

'On target. Infection, returns. Benzothoractine, cannot stop.'

'From what I have heard, things left inside wounds support infection. Bullets, arrows, those sorts of things.'

'PLR, no bullets.'

'PLR?'

'Plasma Lance Rifle. Fires shaped plasma, electro-inductive field collapse, utilising. Armour, k-mail interlock, of uniform, stopped shot, almost.'

'Fox, I did not understand any of that, but what

I want to know is whether you have checked in the wound?'

'No need.'

'So you have not.'

'Irrelevant!' snapped Fox, suddenly agitated.

BC's eyes flickered open.

'FoxS3, attention!' said BC hoarsely.

Immediately Fox snapped to attention and gave his odd salute again. BC shook his head, then sat up.

'Consider. Myself, holding wound, forcing, k-mail interlock cloth fragments, into wound, from uniform, possibly. Target: clean wound.'

'Target acquired!'

'Miss Emily?' asked BC.

'Yes?' asked Emily breathlessly.

'Yourself, battlefield surgery, training, have?'

Emily was nearly wrenched in two, partly by pride at being mistaken for a battlefield nurse, and partly by the shame of what her answer had to be.

'No, but I know how to make fires, and that one should sterilise things in boiling water for an operation.'

'Do so,' wheezed BC, laying back.

Emily turned to Daniel and Barry.

'You two are going to help,' she stated.

'Me?' asked Barry.

'Blood makes me faint,' said Daniel.

'Who are these coves?' asked Barry. 'I mean, I know some dodgy rogers, but these two are bloody dangerous.'

'They are soldiers who are on our side, and they need our help.'

'Our side?' asked Daniel. 'I thought Fox is Norwegian.'

'You heard what BC said. They are from the British Imperial SYS-IK Cadets.'

'Talks like a foreigner,' observed Barry.

'That's to fool spies,' improvised Emily. 'Look, we have to save BC! Understand? He needs help now!'

'But what can we do?' asked Barry.

'Fetch, carry, and follow orders. *You* can go out and find a cooking pot. A large cooking pot! Go! Move! Daniel, not you.'

'What should I do then?' asked Daniel.

'Start a fire. I know you can do that.'

Over the course of the next hour Daniel got a fire going in a grate in a corner of the room, using broken pieces of packing cases. Barry returned with a cooking pot that he appeared to have stolen from somewhere nearby. While the improvised surgical instruments were being cleaned, and the waxed thread was soaking in an iodine solution, Fox made an operating table out of packing cases. The room echoed oddly, allowing distant conversations to be overheard, Emily now realised. She listened to Daniel and Barry whispering, and she did not like what she heard.

'Dan Man, did we say we'd help?' asked Barry.

'Ah, can't recall agreeing to.'

'Then what are we doin'?'

'Following orders. Emily's orders.'

'Why?'

'Because when Emily says jump, you just say "How high?", whether you feel like jumping or not.'

'Those coves ain't British.'

'Emily thinks they are.'

'She's daft.'

'Perhaps she knows something that we don't.'

'Ya reckon?'

'Yes, I suppose.'

'Secret British soldiers. Er, suppose we'd better give a hand then, but I still don't like it.'

At last, kneeling beside the packing case platform, Fox began to cut through the bandages, all the while listing things that he needed.

'Medicinal alcohol, jars, pot of boiling water, bandages, tincture of iodine, potash of permanganate, bicarbonate of soda, darning needles, wax thread, twelve candles, three mirrors,' he said slowly and clearly. 'Emily, Daniel, Barry, lay out, have ready.'

Fox had the last of the improvised bandaging cut away and had cleaned BC's abdomen by the time Emily returned. Revealed was inflamed flesh and charred skin, along with tatters of cloth and congealed blood. Emily reeled. Barry caught her and guided her to beside Daniel, who was sitting on the floor with his hands over his eyes. The ashen-faced Barry knelt beside Fox, and began passing things as they were needed. Only BC's stomach was visible.

'Must operate,' said Fox. 'Emily, on target. In wound, char, cloth, causing infection. Must remove.'

'Why did you not do that earlier?' asked Emily.

'Diagnosis wrong,' said BC. 'Thought, benzo-thoractine alone, enough. Operation, last resort. Thought, needing, only last, to NineFive.'

'Water, boiled, needing,' said Fox.

'I shall fetch it,' whispered Emily, who then got up, dashed out to the window and vomited her breakfast into the guttering space between the roofs. After five very deep breaths she had a grip on herself again, and slowly tottered back to collect the pot of boiling water.

To Emily's considerable surprise, BC made no sound at all as the charred cloth and dried blood were soaked and eased away with damp swabs, then the dead skin was cut from his wound. Emily kept thinking that a splinter in her finger from the firewood was her worst injury for as long as she could remember. A messy pile of debris slowly built up in a tin pan beside Fox. Barry began to feed it into the fire. The scent of burning cloth and flesh hung heavily on the air, and the steam from the hot water condensed on the peeling wallpaper. Finally Fox took out a kit no bigger than Emily's thumb and began mixing tiny amounts of crystals into some type of lotion.

'What's the coloured goo, guv?' asked Barry, holding a jar as Fox spread a blue paste on the edge of the wound with a salt spoon.

'Thorenzaline-dermo-bethanalide, skin, stretching, for purpose of, wounds, sewing,' replied Fox.

At this point Daniel fainted. Barry dragged his friend over to the window, and looked relieved to have something to do that removed him from what was happening on the improvised table. Emily knelt beside Fox as he worked.

It was only when Fox was preparing to bandage BC again that Emily realised what was odd about his body. It looked like the paintings of the Greek and Roman gods, because the muscles stood out hard and firm beneath the skin, yet that skin was smooth and hairless. This brought home to Emily how very young BC really was, yet there were scars here and there, and on the lower rib cage was the mark of an old burn the size of Emily's palm. A battle-hardened child, thought Emily. What sort of army has battle-hardened children? At last the bandaging was done, and Fox sat back on his heels. BC lay limp.

'Danny boy, all over,' said Barry, who was kneeling beside Daniel. 'You can open yer eyes now.'

It was only noon by the time the operation had been completed. As BC lay resting, Fox fed the remaining evidence of the operation into the fire, and Barry left to steal lunch for them. By the time some clock tower was ringing out two o'clock, BC decreed that it was time to go to wherever they were taking him.

'Your, ah, home?' he asked Emily. 'Can stay? Recover?'

'We would have to explain you to my parents,' said Emily, admitting to what was quite a serious problem.

'That could be awkward,' agreed Daniel.

'Oi, my old man wouldn't notice if his bum had been stolen,' announced Barry. 'BC, mate of mine, ya can stay in the parcels room at the station. That way one of us could always be to hand, in case ya has a turn.'

'Turn?' asked BC.

'That means to become ill very suddenly,' said Emily.

'To train, as is, BC, to walk, difficult,' Fox pointed out. 'Must carry.'

'So what's the problem?' asked Barry.

'To carry, need reason.'

'No problem there, Foxy.'

Soon BC had his trouser leg rolled up and a bandage around his ankle. This declared to everyone that he could not walk because of some minor accident, and so had to be carried.

'Now then, Fox, can you carry BC to the station?' asked Emily.

'Undignified,' protested Fox. 'Battle Commander, is.'

'Fox, listen to me, this is a good plan,' insisted

Emily. 'Can you carry BC to the railway station?'

'Yes.'

'Well then, do so!'

'Oh lor, this is stranger than some of old Aitkinson's French postcards,' said Barry unhappily.

Into Barry's bag went the small collection of strange objects from beside BC's improvised bed.

'Of that, take care,' said Fox, indicating the plasma lance rifle. 'Dangerous weapon.'

'Very dangerous weapon,' added BC.

'Look, er, I don't think I'm, like, qualified to carry this sorta stuff,' Barry said.

'You *will* carry it as your duty to the British Empire, and that's the end of it!' ordered Emily. 'Fox, pick up BC. Danny, you will open doors and buy tickets. If anyone tries to stop us, I shall deal with them.'

With that Fox swept BC up, Daniel opened the door, and then they were on their way.

'How far could you carry BC if we have to walk further than the station?' asked Emily as they descended the stairs.

'As needed, so far,' replied Fox.

They were barely out of the door when the gang that had robbed Daniel appeared from an alleyway nearby. The youths began to spread out.

'Wot's 'ere, then?' said one wearing an oversize cap. 'It's dirty little boy an' all.'

'Got 'is own push,' said a rather thick-set youth with a cigarette at one corner of his mouth.

'Then that's another push in our parish,' said the youth in the cap, who appeared to be their leader. 'Gotta teach 'em wot 'appens to invaders.'

Three of the five had knives out by now, and one had a cane. Emily drew breath for a scream, then caught herself. Within Barry's bag was a weapon that could kill them all in moments ... but that seemed like going too far. She could threaten them with it, but to them it would look like a toy, so they would not take it seriously until it was too late. On the other hand, she also had Fox.

'Fox, threat, remove!' barked Emily, hardly realising that the words were leaving her lips.

In a single, fluid movement, Fox turned and draped BC over Daniel, then kept turning and swept his foot up to strike the knife hand of the nearest youth. The knife went spinning out of sight. Meantime Daniel collapsed under BC's weight, striking his head against a brick wall. Emily turned back to Fox in time to see him cross his arms to ensnare the descending blow from the cane while striking out with a kick that was more like a punch to catch another youth in the face. Having secured the cane, he drove the butt up into the jaw of its owner. Incredibly, BC had somehow summoned the energy to fight too. A delicate flick of his foot sent a push boy's knife spinning away, then a strange, flat kick to the stomach doubled him over with a thud like a sledgehammer driving fence posts. With a curiously graceful hop-step, he darted forward to take the youth by the hair before driving a knee into the side of his face. The youth collapsed.

A push boy tried to pin Fox from behind. Fox dropped his weight and ran backwards, slamming the youth against a wall. Fox now twisted free, pinned his attacker's arm and snapped one of his fingers, so that he shrieked with pain. Emily saw the two other gang members huddling together, wide-eyed with fear. One of them was taking out a little pistol.

'Fox, gun!' warned Emily, and Fox somehow flipped the youth he was holding through the air, to bring him crashing down on his friend with the gun. Fox closed with him, and his elbow crashed into the youth's jaw with a loud snap.

By now the fifth member of the push was out of the lane and gone. Emily glanced around. BC was leaning against a wall and panting heavily. Daniel shook his head and blinked his eyes. Barry was backed against a wall, clutching his bag, his mouth hanging open. Fox was uncurling from a crouch, still holding the cane and wary of whether or not there was still a threat.

'Emily, gun, collect,' panted BC.

Emily picked up the little pistol − and the fifth member of the gang reappeared, with three police-men.

'That's 'im, that's the cove wot's murderin' me mates!' cried the youth.

Emily thought very fast. Explaining all of this

to the police would involve her parents finding out about their adventure. Worse, Fox would probably have to make statements to magistrates, have to produce papers that he did not have, explain where he came from … and worst of all, have to prove it. As for the problems that accounting for BC would involve, it did not bear thinking about. Emily made her decision, then thought, Am I being a bad girl or a great leader?

'Fox, attack!' she barked.

The cane whirled into Emily's field of vision to strike the leading policeman on the forehead. Even as Fox charged the man beside him, BC flung something at the third policeman, who dropped his baton and clutched at Mr Lang's letter opener, which had embedded itself in his shoulder. Fox swept his foot into the back of a knee, collapsing the policeman so that he struck the back of his head against a wall. By now the remaining policeman had pulled the letter opener from his shoulder, and attempted to threaten BC with it. BC brought his hands down on the policeman's wrist with his fingers splayed wide, spun his entire body around so that the man's arm was twisted up behind his back, then elbowed him on the side of the head. He collapsed.

The fifth member of the push had watched all of this with his eyes bulging, and once again he turned to run. He found his escape blocked by Emily. She was holding the push captain's pistol in both hands.

'You just put your hands up, you horrid little boy,' declared Emily in the most menacing voice that she could manage.

With no visible emotion whatsoever, Fox seized him by the collar and slashed downwards with his strange little knife. The youth's clothing peeled away neatly, leaving him standing in just his boots and socks. Fox pointed down into the alley from where the push had emerged.

'Hide!' he ordered.

The youth ran and hid. Emily tried to work out whether she was feeling more traumatised from holding a gun for the very first time, or from having seen her very first naked boy. Fox took Mr Lang's letter opener from the unconscious policeman's hand, wiped the blood from the blade, and handed it back to BC. BC was on his feet, but leaning against a wall and looking unsteady. He turned his disturbingly sharp eyes on Emily.

'Safety catch, release, next time,' BC commented, waving the letter opener at Emily's gun. 'On trigger, place finger, also. Not trigger guard. Returning dagger, yours. Nice balance.'

Before another quarter minute was past, the five of them were out of the lane, again with Fox carrying BC. They had reached Flinders Street Station and were sitting on a bench by the time police whistles began sounding in the distance.

'Do you think we shall be arrested?' asked Daniel nervously.

'Nah, the coppers will say they 'ad a stoush with that push, and that they won,' said Barry, whose nerve seemed to be returning. 'Scabby coves will get arrested.'

'Serves them right for robbing me the other day,' said Daniel.

'You never told me that!' cried Emily.

'Train's comin',' said Barry, hoping to prevent raised voices that would draw attention to them.

'BC, can you walk to board the train?' asked Emily as she stood up.

'Asleep,' said Fox. 'Will carry.'

After all that had happened in the city, the train journey was remarkable for the fact that nothing happened at all. Barry's father was busy selling tickets at their home station, so that it was no problem to hide BC in one of the small storerooms.

'The old man thinks stores is too much like 'ard work, so I does it all after school,' explained Barry. 'Come Christmas, I'm outta school for good an' in me career.'

Emily and Daniel went home for blankets and a pillow, and when they returned Emily made up one of the shelves as a bunk. BC had been lying in a corner on old mailbags, but now he sat up and shook his head.

'Somnulacillian, two tabs,' he said to Fox, who turned to Barry.

'Bag,' Fox said softly.

Barry produced his bag, and from this Fox took all of the strange things from the room in Flinders Lane. This included the tiny kit of medical supplies. He dissolved two pinhead-sized tablets in a glass of water, which BC drank, then he lifted the youth onto the bunk and put the stubby rifle in his hands. BC lay back and closed his eyes.

'Healing coma, twenty-five, induction of,' he explained.

'What's he mean?' Barry asked Emily.

'The tablets will make BC sleep, um, so that he heals faster,' Emily guessed.

'Oi, with all the sleepin' me old man docs, you'd think he'd be the fittest cove in Melbourne,' replied Barry, then he raised his finger at the sound of a distant bell. 'Train comin'. I gotta do the gates, now I'm 'ere. Back soon.'

Neither Emily nor Daniel said much while Barry was gone. Fox busied himself with tidying his tiny medical kit and other supplies, and occasionally checked BC's pulse. Presently Barry returned.

'Bad news,' he announced. 'Lurker was in the dogbox on that train.'

'And who is Lurker?' Emily interjected, by now feeling vaguely annoyed about something, but not

sure what it was or what to do about it. 'If it's that
horrid Lurker the Worker –'

'Yeah, it's him. Lurker lurks around and hears stuff,
like. Anyhow, Lurker heard that a station inspection's
on Wednesday. We gotta have BC out by then ... for
a day, anyhow.'

'But he cannot be moved!' protested Emily.

'Benzothoractine, one tab, in reserve,' announced
Fox. 'Battle-ready, renders, duration, five hours.'

'Um, so you have a medicine that allows BC to
walk about normally for five hours?' asked Emily
after thinking about the words.

'Did say.'

It was now that BC turned over on the bunk and
opened his eyes.

'FoxS3, Barry, Daniel, leave,' he said softly, his
voice already slurred with the sleeping mixture.

Having been given an order, Fox walked straight
out. Barry and Daniel took their lead from Fox, and
filed out behind him. Now BC turned to Emily.

'Must speak, ah ...' Strain twisted BC's face, and
for a moment Emily thought he resembled the boys
trying to gather the courage to ask her for a dance
at the school balls that she attended. BC actually
looked embarrassed. 'Must speak, courtly!' was what
BC finally forced himself to say. 'Is like, your speech,
being. No alternative, complex matters, must explain.
Battle standard, is limited. Scholarly, too complex.
Speaking courtly, is presumption. Apologies. No

choice. Important thing, to ask.'

'BC, please, speak courtly,' said Emily. 'I'll never tell anyone.'

BC closed his eyes, then lay still for some time. Finally he turned his head on the pillow, opened his eyes, and stared unblinking at Emily.

'You must understand, this is unimaginably embarrassing for me,' BC whispered in English that was close to flawless. 'I am stepping out of my role as a battle commander, and being BC is all that I have left.'

'Oh no, you have me!' babbled Emily, then immediately wished that she had said nothing. 'I am your friend,' she added hastily, hoping that he would not get the wrong idea.

'Friend,' echoed BC. 'That word is forbidden to the battle, scholar, and command classes. I am of the command class, we are born to lead. We speak courtly because we must kneel before the nobles and royalty, as well as stand with soldiers.'

'I never knew it was like this in Britain,' breathed Emily.

'I am not from Britain as you know it, neither is Fox. I am from a place ... that does not exist. Should fortune smile upon us, it will never exist. In that place, I was made a Deputy Boat Commander at the age of seven, and a Boat Commander two years later. When I was just eleven years of age I was promoted to become the youngest Battle Commander in history. I was to be presented with the Imperial Youth Cross by King Charles himself.'

'You speak so well,' said Emily when BC paused for breath.

'Thank you Miss, you are very kind. I speak D-field, D-tech, D-comm, and D-regal, of course, and I speak the ally languages French, Spanish and Japanese as well.'

'What are the D languages?' asked Emily, her head whirling and her mind barely assimilating the strangeness that she was hearing.

'They are the German versions of battle standard, scholarly, and courtly. The BBC tutorvids say that the Germans stole the idea of language classes from us, but who can know what the truth may be? The Germans have a command language too, but we do not. I can only apologise for speaking to you this way, but as you must be aware, I have no choice. In your world, everyone speaks courtly. I find it profoundly unsettling.'

'Please, don't feel bad!' insisted Emily. 'This is Victoria, even someone as uncouth as Barry is allowed to speak, er, courtly.'

BC's head fell back on the pillow as the somnulacillian's effect washed through his mind.

'Why is he called Barry the Bag?' he asked, his mind losing focus and his voice slurred.

'Oh, because of that horrid, tatty bag he carries everywhere. All sorts of things vanish into it, such as bottles of my father's wine. As for what comes out, well!'

'Well?'

'He has French postcards. They are unimaginably naughty!'

'Why should postcards from our occupied French allies be naughty?'

'I ...'

Words failed Emily. She lived in a world where one had to say *postcard from France* if one meant a French postcard that was actually not rude. She searched for words to describe what everyone should know.

'They have pictures of ladies – well, women – who are wearing no clothes,' she managed at last.

'Is that because they are very poor?' asked BC innocently, all the while fighting to stay awake.

'No!' snapped Emily, again exasperated and floundering for words.

Suddenly Emily realised what BC must be going through, having to speak courtly. In his society, this was probably the rudest thing possible. Emily took a deep breath. If BC could cope with embarrassment, she could too.

'The women are showing their bottoms and titties,' she managed. 'Boys like to look at them. They are called French postcards, but I am sure that some of the girls are Australians just pretending to be French.'

'Ah, bonding revels,' said BC, who seemed to be struggling with the concept of what it meant to be rude.

'Bonding revels?' asked Emily.

'Yes. The seats do it, once they are over twelve years of age. Everyone gets a turn at taking off their clothes and dancing on a table while others throw food, and laugh and cheer.'

'Oh!' gasped Emily, shocked almost speechless. 'Did, er, you ever do it?'

'I am command class. It is my place to attend bonding revels, but not to participate.'

The onslaught of alien values was by now on the very edge of what Emily could cope with. Her head spinning, she sat down heavily on a large package. He is a different person when he speaks in courtly, thought Emily. Something about that hard, precise, unforgiving battle standard language gives those who speak it a focus and intensity that is almost a weapon by itself.

'You said you had something important to ask me,' prompted Emily.

'Ah, my apologies,' said BC, his voice slurring again. 'The allure of speaking courtly ... and the pain from the operation has ... muddled my thoughts. Nearly asleep, but must tell you ... save last benzothoractine tablet ... in case I have to fight ... or you must ...'

'Fight?' gasped Emily. 'You will do no such thing! Not until you are well enough, anyway.'

'You have ... soul of command,' said BC in a soft, slow whisper. 'Can you understand ... what is meant ... to accept ... CW ... and hear mission profile?'

'With all my heart!' said Emily eagerly, realising that she was finally to learn the truth about her enigmatic new friends.

'DBC ... take CW,' whispered BC, holding up the strange, stubby rifle. 'Thumb ... red pad.'

Emily took the weapon with great care, then placed her right thumb on a red, halfpenny-sized patch. It had a rough feel to it.

'Zeta, seven, dash, alpha, delta, six, six, phi, dash, share,' said BC, forcing himself to stay awake for a few moments more. 'Is ... red light ... shining?'

'Yes.'

'Remove thumb ... act with wisdom. I must now ... stand before ... the House of Death. Should the door open ... all ... up to you ...'

BC finally surrendered to the onset of the healing coma. Still holding the oddly light rifle, Emily went to the door and called the others back. Barry and Daniel stared in surprise at the rifle in Emily's hands, but Fox showed no emotion at all.

Fox said, 'To store, groceries, selling, going now. Work, commencing, noon.'

'Wait. Fox, can you explain what BC said to me just now?' asked Emily. 'He gave me this, he called it a CW, and called me DBC. He made a red light come on for me whenever I touch the red pad.'

'Arming light, to fire, is ready, when glowing. This, intensity slide. Low, singe paper. High, cut six inch steel. To you, assigned. Of command, symbolic.'

'Assigned? What do you mean?'

'CW, meaning, Command Weapon. To you, assigned, ranking, Deputy Battle Commander.'

'Fox, please. Can you explain all that again?'

Fox raised his eyes to the ceiling for a moment. 'Shall try.'

Emily sat miserably on her bed, contemplating the stubby rifle that lay on the dresser in front of her row of dolls and bears. DBC. Deputy Battle Commander. BC had conferred the rank upon her, then lapsed into a coma before he could explain anything else. Fox had been no help at all when she had questioned him about what BC had called the 'mission profile'. Briefing was not his duty, apparently. He had, however, explained that the rifle's most powerful setting could cut through the steel armour of a battleship. Lower settings were used when fighting people, so that innocent bystanders or equipment would not be damaged.

'I have command of a soldier from somewhere that does not seem to exist but seems to be British, my younger brother and Barry the Bag,' Emily told the dolls and bears. 'Oh, and I have to lead them on a mission that I know nothing about.'

She recalled the previous day's preparations for battle, which had involved running up and down the stairs to get fit, and arming herself with her father's letter opener. All that suddenly seemed laughably silly, now that she had a gun that could apparently sink a ship. A very big ship. On the other hand, she had no idea who to point it at, or when to use it. Emily cringed at the memory of pointing the pistol at the push boy without removing the safety catch or even putting her finger on the trigger. Suddenly remembering where the pistol had gone, she reached under her dress and took it out.

'It would never do for Martha to find this in the washing,' muttered Emily as she put the little gun beside the plasma lance rifle.

Mission profile. The two words had suddenly become the bane of Emily's life. Clearly BC considered that she could do something called the mission, but BC was lying in a coma with Fox watching over him. Fox was unwilling to discuss the mission profile, because it was not his place. The following day BC would either awake, or be dead, that much he had communicated to Emily. If he awoke, she would learn the mission profile. Until then, what?

Trying not to make a fool of herself was high on Emily's list of priorities, but beyond that there were her duties as DBC. She had command of the squad, but no idea of what to do with it.

'Well, I shall hold it together until BC can take over again,' she declared aloud.

Daniel was her most immediate problem. He had been very annoyed to learn that she had been given command of a squad that he did not recall joining in the first place. Barry was less of a problem, because he tended to assume that anyone doing something vaguely suspicious deserved his help. Fox, of course, accepted her because BC had declared her to be the leader.

Suddenly Emily had it! She was very good at chess. She excelled at strategy and tactics, and leaders needed to be good at strategy and tactics. *That* was why BC had chosen her. She always planned ahead. Emily decided to go to her brother's bedroom and explain that she was only supposed to make decisions, and that all the heroics were to be performed by himself and Barry. That would make him happier, and with luck he might follow her orders.

Emily picked up the command weapon as a symbol of authority, mentally rehearsed what she would say to her brother, and had got as far as his bedroom door when she heard Barry's voice.

'Look, I know it's a bit of a shock, but that's the way it is!' said Barry in a stern but soft manner.

'It's too disgusting!' replied her brother in an unsteady voice. 'Mother once told me that the midwife brings babies in her suitcase. When she puts one in hot water it comes to life.'

'That's horseshit, Danny Boy.'

'Well, have you ever seen anyone doing it?'

'Look, what do ya think dogs are doin' when ya see them playing wheelbarrows in the street?'

'I – come to think of it, people get really embarrassed about dogs doing that, and even throw buck-
ets of water over them,' Daniel conceded.

'That's why grown-ups don't like boys and girls
bein' left alone.'

'But Mother never complains about Emmy and
me being alone together.'

'That's because brothers and sisters don't do it!
Only folk from other families do.'

'But, but why did the groom do it with Martha?
Did they want a baby?'

'Nah, it just feels good. Real, real good.'

'How would you know?'

'Trust me, Danny Boy. Barry the Bag says nothing to incriminate himself, inside a court of law, or
outside.'

'But Martha has not had a baby.'

'It doesn't always happen, not sure why. Ya know,
girls think it's the most lovey-dovey thing they can do
with a cove, so they risk having a baby just to impress
him, like.'

'So that's what Father meant when he said Martha
was seduced. No, I can't believe it, I can't imagine
Martha and the groom playing wheelbarrows.'

'Danny Boy, what would you say if you saw it in
a book?'

'Well ... what is in books is true, unless they are
novels.'

'Good, because guess what Barry has in his bag.'

Emily heard the sound of rummaging.

'*A Scientific Guide to Human Reproductive —*' began Daniel.

'Forget that, just turn to page thirty-seven.'

'Page thirty-seven ... Oh my goodness!'

By now Emily could feel perspiration trickling from her armpits and down her ribcage. All thoughts of the mission profile and leadership disputes had been wiped from her mind while she had listened in on Barry the Bag's private tutorial on human sexuality, but now she climbed back out of the chasm of absolute and complete shock and began composing plans and strategies. Placing her thumb on the red pad of the command weapon, Emily flung her brother's bedroom door open just as the two boys inside had begun giggling.

For a moment there was chaos. Daniel and Barry tossed the book between each other in a bizarre sort of ball game, but at Emily's command 'Raise your hands!' the book was allowed to fall to the floor.

'I can explain,' said Daniel.

'Do so,' replied Emily.

'Well, er, but not just now.'

'Move back, both of you!' snapped Emily.

The two boys backed away until they were stopped by Daniel's bookcase. Emily went down on one knee and snatched up the book. Holding it in one hand, she flipped to page thirty-seven. Upon page thirty-seven was a series of rather graphic line drawings, and the blush that blazed over Emily's cheeks burned like a facecloth that had been dipped in near-boiling water. Daniel and Barry exchanged worried glances.

Tucking the book under her arm, Emily reached out for Barry's bag.

'Barry the … Barry, just what is your proper name?' she asked.

'Barry Porter. I got a middle name like Danny Boy has, but me mum died when I was little, and me old man was at the pub when I was christened, so he never told me.'

'Didn't your mum run off with a fishmonger from South Melbourne when you were thirteen?' said Daniel.

'You said you'd never tell!' shouted Barry, rounding on Daniel.

'But –'

'Anyway, she won't see me, so she might as well be dead.'

'You said you can't go to their shop because you stole ten shillings when you went there last month and the fishmonger said he would wring your neck if he ever caught –'

'Enough!' cried Emily. 'Barry Porter, swear that you accept my position as Deputy Battle Commander, or I shall empty your bag onto the dining room table in front of my mother and father.'

'Oh shit, no, no, that's got all me artistic postcards, an' special keys, and, er, rubber medical devices of a highly personal nature, and –'

'Swear!'

'Swear? Er, wot ya mean? Shit? Bugger? Friggin' 'ell?'

'Barry, just say "I swear",' advised Daniel.

'I swear,' said Barry.

'Splendid,' said Emily, turning to Daniel. 'Daniel Edward Lang, unless I have your sworn word that you accept my position as Deputy Battle Commander, I shall go straight downstairs, present this book to Mother and Father, and open it at page thirty-seven.'

Once again Daniel and Barry exchanged worried glances, this time augmented by hopeless shrugs.

'I swear,' said Daniel.

'Good,' said Emily. 'Now I am going to impound this book and bag at least until tomorrow evening, when BC is awake again. Until then, you two will obey my orders, just as if I were a captain in an army, and you were common soldiers.'

As she returned to her room, Emily was certain that her shame of earlier in the day had been wiped out. She might not be able to command the loyalty that people gave BC, and she certainly did not have his charisma, but she definitely had ways of getting people to do what she ordered. If she were not able to lead BC's squad against whoever the enemy might be, she would certainly hand it back to him intact and ready for action.

4

SPY

It was the following morning, over breakfast, that Emily made her announcement. Daniel had made the mistake of allowing himself to feel a little relaxed. After all, his sister was in charge now, so when they were caught and put on trial he could blame her for blackmailing him with *A Scientific Guide to Human Reproductive Biology*. Mrs Lang had just proposed that Fox be invited over for dinner that night when Daniel noticed his sister smile ominously for a moment, then relax her face into a perfect blank.

This is it. I know that look. Page thirty-seven is about to cut off my pocket money forever and get my bottom caned until it glows in the dark, thought Daniel.

'Did you know that one of Fox's officers is in Melbourne?' asked Emily.

'An officer?' exclaimed Mrs Lang at once. 'Do you think he might come to dinner as well?'

Daniel sagged with relief, and did not spare a thought for Emily's possible motive for telling her mother about BC. Page thirty-seven was not going to be mentioned, nothing else in all the world was as important as that.

'Fox says that he is not very well, that he was injured in some fight with mutineers.'

'Oh dear, is he confined to bed?'

'Fox did not say, but he will be working at the grocery store today, so I can ask him after school, when Martha is walking me home.'

It was not often that Daniel looked forward to going to school, but on this particular Tuesday he could not get out of the house fast enough. Barry was at the railway station, taking one of his frequent days off from his own school.

'I'm mindin' BC an' all,' he muttered conspiratorially through the ticket window grille. 'Foxy Boy has gone early to deliver for Aitkinson.'

'So BC is still alive?' asked Daniel.

'Warm and breathin', reckon that's alive. Lor, but I feel naked wi'out me bag.'

'Emily seems to have kept the bag and the book hidden so far. You had better really look after BC, so he can take over again and we can get everything back.'

'First time in me life I've thought about goin' to the coppers. All this got the wind up me.'

'Will you?' asked Daniel, who was also feeling increasingly nervous about Fox and BC.

'Nah, not yet. Never live it down if word got out that Barry the Bag asked a copper for help.'

Daniel's school day passed slowly, and he had trouble concentrating on anything at all, but his class was let out early due to some ceremony practise for the opening of parliament. Just after four o'clock he stepped off the train again, and as usual Barry was collecting tickets. Daniel waited until everyone else had left the platform.

'Ha ha, young squire, d'ya have a tikky today?' Barry called, although he was not smiling.

'No, some push stole it!' muttered Daniel, waving his ticket at Barry. 'How is BC?'

'Awake, and Foxy Boy is in with 'im. Yer sister is there too, an' they're arguin'.'

'Arguing? About what?'

'That benny-thorry-something medicine. Emmy thinks BC should have the last tablet now.'

'But why?'

'Search me bag, Danny Boy, I don't know. It had better be to do with getting BC out of the storeroom before the inspector arrives tomorrow, though. Oh, and yer bossy sister said we was to come in as soon as ya got off the train.'

Daniel and Barry entered the parcels store in time

to see Fox hand a large pile of coins over to BC.

'Cor, how'd ya 'alf inch that lot from old Aitkinson?' exclaimed Barry before he could stop himself.

'Half inch?' asked BC.

'Pinch,' translated Emily, who then added, 'it's rhyming slang for "steal".'

'No theft,' said Fox as he held up a thin, silvery tube. 'Legitimate salvage, at beach, mine detector, usage for, metal detection.'

'Was I supposed to understand that?' asked Barry.

'That tube detects coins under the sand,' explained Emily. 'Fox spent his lunchtime at the beach and collected the worth of fifteen pounds in lost coins.'

'Trade ya that for everythin' in me bag!' offered Barry at once.

Emily put a finger to her lips, then turned to BC. BC scanned the four of them, before turning back to Emily.

'Daniel, Barry, loyal?' he asked.

'Loyal but doubtful,' said Emily. 'They obey me out of fear.'

Like everyone else, thought Daniel.

'Daniel, Barry, need demonstration, as discussed,' said BC. 'PLR. Sheer power, will convince, before explaining, who are.'

'Tactically dangerous,' advised Fox.

'Strategically vital,' countered BC. 'Danny, Barry, must convince.'

'Give me a half hour,' said Emily, picking up a large knitting bag. 'Danny, Barry, come with me.'

❁

Emily, Daniel and Barry took the next train south. Emily said nothing on the short trip, but sat cradling her large knitting bag with cane handles. At South Brighton they got off, and Emily led them toward the nearby beach.

'Hurry, I want to catch the train as it returns from Sandringham,' said Emily.

'What are we doing?' asked Daniel.

'You two are doing nothing. I, on the other hand, am showing you something.'

Holloway Bend was a small bay, and a little back from the beach were mounds of shells and charcoal where the natives had roasted shellfish for hundreds of years before European settlement. These were overgrown with bushes now, and it was in the shelter of the bushes that Emily knelt down, opened her bag, and drew out the odd, vaguely gun-shaped weapon that BC had entrusted to her. Daniel watched as she made some adjustments to it.

'See that buoy a few hundred yards out to sea?' she said, pointing the weapon without really aiming it.

'Yes,' replied Daniel.

'Shouldn't ya look through the sights?' asked Barry.

Emily pressed the firing stud. There was the sharp, shrill squeak. An area of water about a hundred yards across in the general vicinity of the buoy erupted skywards, and moments later a wall of sound like a thunderclap going off in a toilet cubicle rolled over them. When Daniel and Barry finally turned back to Emily, she had returned the weapon to her bag and was standing up. By the look on her face, Daniel decided, even she had not realised just how powerful the weapon really was. Those promenading along the beachfront who had not started running when the sea had exploded now scampered for higher ground as a wave about two yards high crashed onto the beach. Salty water began to shower down on them out of a clear sky.

'Hurry boys, the train will be returning soon,' Emily said in a breathless whisper, as the echoes of the blast reverberated around them.

As they left, Daniel glanced back out to sea. Out on the choppy maelstrom of water, the buoy was still intact. They were hurrying across the Esplanade before Daniel was able to speak again.

'What is that thing?' he asked.

'A weapon, obviously. BC asked me to demonstrate it to you. He wanted you to be convinced.'

'I'm convinced!' babbled Barry.

'Convinced about what?' asked Daniel.

'Convinced that BC and Fox are very, very special people, and are to be taken seriously.'

'I didn't need no convincin' about that,' said Barry. 'Oi, there's the train, we'd better run.'

People who had not been on the beach were now running in that direction and pointing excitedly at the cloud of steam and water that was towering over the bay. Those who had been on the beach, however, were running inland, and advising everyone else to do so. Nobody paid any attention to Emily, Daniel and Barry. Why should they? thought Daniel. How could three schoolchildren possibly cause an explosion of that size? We would need a gun as big as a steam train to do that ... or something worse.

Having returned to North Brighton Station, Emily shepherded the boys in to see BC.

'They are convinced,' declared Emily, gesturing to Daniel and Barry.

'Agree, then,' replied BC.

Daniel did not understand all that was going on, but it was clear that his sister had negotiated something with BC. It was equally clear that Barry and he were to be involved.

'BC will now declare his mission profile in courtly English,' Emily explained. 'Do *not* laugh. Speaking as we do is a very difficult thing for BC.'

Although he was lying on his side on a parcel sorting shelf, to Daniel BC still had the charisma of a ballroom jammed full of generals. He spent some moments looking awkward, however. Courtly English was clearly not to be spoken casually, wherever he came from.

'All of you are British?' he asked softly, although his voice had all the menace of the safety catch on one of Mr Lang's guns clicking free.

'Yes,' replied Emily. Daniel nodded.

'Am I?' hissed Barry to Daniel.

'Yes.'

'Er, yeah,' Barry finally declared. 'That is, yes.'

'Good, because you are required to perform active military service for the British Empire,' continued BC, and Daniel suddenly realised that his English was flawless. 'It is a British Empire that does not exist yet, and if we are successful it will never exist. Do you all agree?'

With Emily in possession of a weapon that could probably take on the entire British Navy with a pretty good chance of winning, plus his most recently acquired scientific textbook, no doubt with a bookmark on page thirty-seven, Daniel felt that he had no choice whatsoever. He and Barry glanced at each other, then said 'Yes' together.

BC's eyes turned to Emily. 'Well?' he asked.

'If you agree to take the benzothoractine, then yes,' she answered.

'I do agree,' replied BC. 'I am forced to trust your judgement in this matter.' He looked to the others. 'I am very weak, and FoxS3 says I must rest for the next seven days. Within the next week the new Australian parliament opens, however, so as you know I have been compelled to appoint a deputy battle commander. Emily Lang is my appointee as Deputy Battle Commander of this crew.'

'Blimey, just what are we?' asked Barry.

Fox flinched at the breach of discipline, but BC waved him silent.

'SYS-IK. Special Youth Service Infiltration Killer crew.'

'Killer?' gasped Barry. 'Ya mean we has to give coves the big push?'

'We have the functions of infiltration, espionage, sabotage and assassination. Are there any more questions?'

'Why did you choose me as deputy?' asked Emily.

'You have initiative and intelligence, cope well with stress, think quickly and can plan ahead.'

'But why not appoint Fox?'

'Fox has been conditioned not to lead. Are there more questions? No? Good, I shall call the seats. I am Liore-BC, and my status is casualty. Emily-DBC is Deputy Battle Commander until I return to active duty, and is also EmilyS4 in stroke. FoxS3 is the cybertech, medical, and infiltration expert, and his assessments are never wrong. DanS2, Daniel, you are brave, but require discipline. Look to FoxS3 as a mentor. You could be a good decoy, but remember that decoys are the first to die.'

Daniel swallowed, then shivered. Heroics were all very well, but not if real danger was involved.

BC's eyes moved on. 'BarryS1, you are a cunning, resourceful and skilled infiltrator. In the days to come we may depend on you a great deal. Your place is bow, but you will be called BarryS1.'

'Er, you got the right Barry?' laughed Barry nervously, glancing around.

'Would all other Barrys present please raise their hands?' asked Emily.

'Could you please explain, I do not understand,' said BC.

'Joke, reduction of tension, for purpose of,' said Emily, mocking battle standard.

'Ah, thank you. Now Barry, Emily tells me that you can be less than honest sometimes. *Never* be dishonest with me. Understand? If you betray us, I shall kill you myself.'

Barry shivered, and Emily went very pale. For some moments Daniel thought that his bladder might fail him. Here was someone who not only killed, he probably did it quite often. BC was definitely not one of those decent, cheery heroes in British adventure novels who always gave the villains a sporting chance. If it came to that, BC was a lot more frightening than even the villains in British adventure novels, yet Daniel felt curiously anxious to have his approval. BC was somehow larger than life, even though there was something distinctly cold and predatory about him.

'Now then, are all of you comfortable with your places?' asked BC.

Nobody was inclined to cross him, least of all Daniel.

'I shall now explain the mission profile,' BC continued, then allowed a long pause for emphasis. 'Long ago, in the year 1901, in the month of May, there was a huge gathering of the courtly and political leaders in Australia, in this very city of Melbourne.'

'But it's 1901 now,' said Barry. 'I'm pretty sure it's May, too.'

'It's still April,' said Emily.

'Patience Barry, just listen and concentrate,' said BC. 'Concentrate, as if your life depends on it.'

'Which it probably does,' whispered Daniel, elbowing Barry.

'The leaders were here to celebrate the Australian colonies joining together as a single nation,' BC went on. 'The biggest, grandest ceremony of all was the opening of the first Australian parliament in the Exhibition Buildings. Do you all know about that?'

'Sorta,' mumbled Barry.

'I know all about that from school,' declared Daniel. 'Father is always saying what a stupid idea Federation is, and how it should be stopped or the British Empire will be ruined, but I think it will be good for Australia.'

'But ... but none of that has happened as yet,' said Emily. 'Parliament opens next week, yet you talk about it like it's in the past.'

'Have you not guessed as yet, Emily-DBC?' asked BC with the slightest suggestion of a smile. 'Fox and I are from the future. The weapon in your knitting bag will not even be invented for another ninety years.'

Judging from the expression on her face, Daniel decided that Emily had not guessed as much. Barry scratched his head, and made it clear that the concept of time travel was a long way beyond his own imagination as well. Daniel, on the other hand, had recently read a story about time travel, and was familiar with the idea.

'Did you build a time machine, like in the story Mr Wells wrote?' asked Daniel.

'The difference between the Wells story and real time travel is greater than the difference between a paper boat and an ocean liner, but the principle is the same,' replied BC. 'FoxS3 and I are from early in the twenty-first century.'

BC allowed them some moments to absorb this. Emily looked either confused, or sceptical, or astounded, or perhaps all three. Barry looked absolutely blank.

Forget true or false, thought Daniel. Why are they here?

'So, why come back?' he asked.

'Because of the opening of parliament. All the most important people in the country, and many from Britain, were gathered under the one roof, but moments before the first Australian parliament was declared in session, a series of explosions brought down that entire roof. The casualties were terrible. Only one in three who were inside was alive by the dawn of the next day. The police who sifted through the rubble found pieces of German military equipment, and their investigations soon uncovered a German conspiracy in the artistic community of Melbourne. Germans posing as artists had hidden explosives in the roof of the Exhibition Buildings, and detonated them to kill everyone. It was a conspiracy to destroy the leadership of Australia, so that hidden warships and troops in Germany's New Guinea colony could invade and take over.'

'You … you mean we shall be invaded?' gasped Emily.

'Do not worry, the Germans did not invade Australia,' BC said. 'But what happened was unimaginably worse. Nearly every British warship that could be mustered was ordered to steam to Australia to stop the invasion. The greatest imperial fleet in history arrived, but there were no German ships to be found. They then invaded the German colony in New Guinea. There were no warships there, either.'

'So they all went home?' asked Daniel.

'No. The Germans now declared war on Britain over the attack on their colony. Because all the British ships were on the other side of the world, Britain was much weakened when the Germans attacked.'

'You mean the Germans won?' asked Daniel, incredulous.

'Yes. The British fleet was rushed back with all possible speed, but they arrived in poor condition after having to steam to the ends of the earth and back with no rest. Suffice to say that the Battle of Portsmouth was a close-fought and savage engagement, but the Germans won. The British fleet was scattered, but luckily only one ship in ten was actually sunk, so it was gradually regrouped. The royal family and most of parliament had been whisked away to Canada early in the invasion, so we had both ships and leaders, even if we did not have Britain. Melbourne was established as the new capital of the British Empire.'

'Oh, so that was good for Australia?' ventured Emily.

'No. International relations have been rather disastrous ever since. There has been a serious war every three or four years for a century, and five of those have been what we call world wars. The whole of the Earth either builds weapons or fights with them. All of the best careers are in the army, navy, air force, and space service.'

'Air force? Space service?' asked Daniel.

'They are like the navy, except that they have metal birds that drop bombs on enemy cities, and which duel with each other in the skies. The world has been strip-mined for a century; the smoke that the factories make is warming the very Earth itself; the polar caps are melting; the sea is rising, and the land is strewn with smashed war machines and graveyards. It is a nightmare, it really is.'

'It sounds very bad,' said Emily, barely able to understand what he had just said, and hoping that her reply was appropriate.

'The world of my time is on the brink of catastrophe, yet everyone is trying their best to tip it over the edge.'

'So Fox and you deserted, and fled into the past?' asked Emily, trying to come to terms with the strange story.

'We did not desert,' said BC firmly. 'We ... had a mission.'

'I know, I saw it!' Emily suddenly burst out, remembering the vision from Fox's cinema machine. 'Fox had a, um, camera thing. I turned it on by accident.'

The expression on BC's face reminded Emily of a mother tiger confronted with a particularly stupid poodle yapping at one of her cubs.

'What did you see?' he asked in a level, flat voice.

'Oh, you and other young people fighting very courageously. You were fighting grown-ups, and were terribly brave. I saw you shot. It must have hurt so much, but you didn't even cry.'

'Cry?' said BC.

'Girls do it,' said Daniel, who was getting tired of

Emily dominating BC's story.

BC shook his head, and seemed to be having trouble gathering his thoughts.

'We all have a duty to the Empire,' he continued. 'For the entire twentieth century the British Empire has been trying to take Britain back from the Germans. When we are not actually having wars, our scientists compete with the German scientists. Australia put a man in space in 1950, then formed the Royal Space Service and put manned bombers into orbit. The Germans then developed a terrible weapon called the atomic bomb. A single such bomb can destroy a city. Next they put them on rockets that could reach anywhere on earth in a half-hour. Our spies stole the secret and we learned to make atomic bombs too, and ... well, that was World War Five. Munich, Bonn, Adelaide, and Capetown were destroyed, but fortunately both sides had only a few atomic bombs each at that time. By 2000, they had built thousands, however, and could have destroyed the entire world about a hundred times over. The talk was that Australia would launch World War Six on the one hundredth anniversary of Germany's attack on Britain. Someone had to do something, or else the world would be destroyed.'

'I cannot imagine anything worse than those terrible bombs,' said Emily.

'There is. Australian scientists invented a time machine. Using it, they planned to send atomic bombs into the past, to destroy German cities with no warning, and before anti-missile systems had been invented. My crew had just won a very important boat race, the most important race of the season in the Empire. Our reward was to be given a part in guarding the time machine as we sent the bombs back in time. Because we were the best of the cadets in the whole empire, we were allowed to be guards so that we could be part of history. As soon as I found out what the time machine was supposed to do ... well, I had a meeting with the crew. We decided to betray our position of trust, and to destroy the time machine before it destroyed the world. My crew, my cadet SYS-IK, attacked the core of the time travel installation. We were nearly wiped out, but we got all the way in and armed a bomb with a timer to destroy it.'

'Could they build another?' asked Emily.

'Nothing is more certain. That is why there was a second part to our plan. If any of us got to the inner chamber, where the controls were located, we were to escape back into the past, to April 1901. If we can stop the original bombing of the first Australian parliament, that terrible century of war will never have happened.'

'Blimey, why didn't the govyment coves send someone official-like back to here, like, to do what yer doin'?' asked Barry.

'Because their whole world is built on war. They

want to win wars, not prevent them. Besides, if they change the distant past, the future they live in will cease to exist.'

'But they would still do that by sending bombs into the past,' said Daniel.

'The generals were going to target 1980, a year when they were already born. Their new selves would then live in a world where Britain had defeated Germany and ruled the world.'

'But then surely you and Fox will cease to exist if you stop the bombing of parliament,' Emily pointed out.

'That is indeed a risk, but being a soldier is a risky business, Emily-DBC. FoxS3 and I are traitors. A century in the future we are the most hated people in the English-speaking world. Please, seven of our crewmates have died for this cause, and Fox and I have disgraced ourselves. Do not let those sacrifices be wasted. Help us as we try to stop our future ever existing.'

BC now filled in some of the background detail in the story of the atrocity that had not yet happened. From the perspective of BC and Fox, history had been quite specific about the conspiracy to bomb Melbourne's Exhibition Buildings, indeed it had been the best researched event in the history of the British Empire. Bombs had been placed around the ceiling

by German agents who had posed as painters in the
Melbourne artistic community for several months.
Having been granted access to the roof in order
to take photographs and make sketches, they had
planted carefully concealed charges, then detonated
them as parliament was about to open. Although the
conspirators were never caught, a search of their
lodgings revealed maps, diagrams, and letters of
instruction written in German.

The addresses of the conspirators were history,
and Fox knew them from memory. On the second
night after he and BC had arrived from the future,
Fox had burgled all five addresses. He found nothing but neatly folded clothes, painting supplies, and
a few sketches and watercolours. On the other hand,
everything was covered in a thin layer of dust. The
rooms were clearly being used as a facade while the
conspirators did their work somewhere else.

There were even stranger discoveries to come,
however. When Fox had stolen into the Exhibition
Buildings and climbed into the recesses and walk-
ways of the roof supports, he had found no trace of
explosives. This was quite perplexing. A century in
the future, every child was taught that bombs had
been planted in the roof weeks before parliament's
opening. As far as Fox could tell, the future seemed
to have changed already.

Little was known of the conspirators. From what
BC said, it was clear that all that he and Fox had to

cling to was that people with German names had rented the five rooms in St Kilda, and that German artists had been circulating in the nearby cafés. Clearly these cafés were their only hope of catching the conspirators, so they would have to be watched.

Because he was the most adult-looking of the crew, BC thought that Fox was a natural choice to monitor the cafés. On the other hand, his speech and accent would attract attention, and he was unfamiliar with the manners and mannerisms of Melbourne in 1901. This rather limited his usefulness as a spy. Finally Barry seemed to decide that he had grasped enough of the situation to make constructive suggestions.

'Er, BC mate, I don't follow most of wot ya said, but ya really reckon there's foreigners attackin' the country?'

'Yes.'

'An' ya reckon yer from what hasn't happened?'

'Yes.'

'But that isn't anywhere. It's from 'ere, except it's gonna happen. You can't come from 'ere if yer already 'ere.'

'Barry, imagine you were to sleep for a hundred years in your bed. Would you feel as if you had travelled into the future when you woke up?'

'Yeah … I see, like that Van Wrinkle cove?'

'Van Winkle,' said Emily.

'Yes, you have it. Now think of a carriage that takes you to that future instead.'

'I think I can. Sorta.'

'All you have to do now is think of a carriage that can move you into the past as well.'

'Oh. So ya got the carriage, like that we can see?'

'No. The time machine is more like a gun. It can shoot things into the past or future, but it stays in its present.'

Barry put his hands to his head, pressing against it as if he were trying to stop it exploding. Daniel knew that look. Barry either did not believe or did not understand.

'Way I sees it, ya workin' for the king,' ventured Barry.

'That is true,' agreed BC.

'Then I'm on yer side. I don't believe all that shit about time carriages, but yer important. I mean any-one that's got a gun that can blow up 'alf the bay just gotta be important. Okay, yer important, so I gotta help.'

'*Can* you help?' asked BC doubtfully.

'Yeah! Mate, ya want to get somethin' dodgy done, ya gotta bring in a professynal. That's where I comes in. I can pretend I'm an artist, and spy on the German artists.'

'Artists tend to be around eighteen or older,' BC pointed out. 'Fox looks eighteen, and Daniel could pass for someone eighteen but thin. You look twelve.'

'Yeah, but that's the whole point, don't ya see? Me and Danny Boy can pretend to be young coves outta school and sellin' artistic postcards.'

'Which is what you will be,' said Emily, disapproval dripping from every word.

'All the better,' said BC, suddenly brightening. 'Barry, explain a little more of what you propose.'

Barry the Bag was very cunning. He did actually have a number of minor burglaries in his past, but because he was what would be called streetwise in a future that did not even exist in the future as yet, he had never been caught. His bag also had a false bottom, so that when the police searched it, they found nothing more than scavenged rubbish and French postcards. Even though Emily had his real bag, Barry quickly improvised a spare, and it was this that he carried as he and Daniel set off on the next train north, along with the station bicycle and BC's instructions of what to look for.

Daniel had a lot to think about as they travelled. BC had put Emily in charge, yet there was no doubt that BC was running everything. Emily just passed on his orders and kept things running when he was asleep.

'Wotcha think of that BC cove?' asked Barry as they travelled. 'Ain't he a worry or wot?'

'A worry?' asked Daniel.

'Yeah, like he said he'd kill me. Don'cha know? Like if I 'ad sixpence for every time the old man said he'd kill me, I'd never have to pick another pocket as long as I lived, but when BC says it, ya know he would.'

'You could try not being dishonest with him,' suggested Daniel.

'Wot? How's I to get by then?'

'You're already dishonest with everyone else.'

'I'm never dishonest with my mate Dan the Man!' declared Barry, patting Daniel on the shoulder.

'What about those three bottles of wine you stole from my father?'

'I only stole two.'

'There were three, Barry. Martha's told Emily about the latest one.'

'Oh, that one. Yeah, I forgot, like in the heat of the emotion.'

'And if I had been BC, you would already be a small pile of ashes that smelled a bit of stale tobacco. This is teamwork, Barry. You are in a team.'

'I've never been in a team.'

'Trust me, in a team you have to think about what's good for everyone, not just yourself.'

'Don't like it,' muttered Barry sullenly.

'Well, do you think I like it? I have to take orders from Emily and not argue back. I hate it, but BC said to, so I do.'

'I thought you was doin' it 'cause she 'as the book on makin' babies. I'm only along 'cause she 'as me bag.'

'At first it was because of that, but not now. I want BC to think I'm, well, all right.'

'At least you got a chance. BC just thinks I'm a scabby little rat who's good at criminal activities, an' he's right.'

'Try hard enough and BC will think you are all right. There's something about him, you just want him to smile because you did well. I do think I would like to die fighting for him.'

Barry shrank away across the bench of the carriage.

'You gotta be jokin'!' he exclaimed. 'Ya mean let yerself be shot off the perch, just so he'd say "Good show" or some daft shit?'

'Yes. I daydream about things like that. I know it sounds strange from someone with a sister like Emmy, but I dream about being a knight fighting hundreds of barbarians so that some girl can escape into a castle.'

'Yeah? Wot then?'

'Well, she looks down from the battlements and cries when I get killed.'

'And that's all?'

'Yes. Don't you dream of being a hero, and dying for girls?'

'Nah, I dreams about gettin' into Madame Plumtree's House of … well, and … I don't dream wot you dream, anyway.'

'I want to die a hero. At first I was frightened by all this business with BC and Fox, but now ... it's like living in a dream.'

'Would ya die for that batty sister of yours?'

'It seems like a waste, but yes. She would have to remember me as a hero.'

'Dan the Man, yer daft! That's a better bet than the favourite in a one-horse race, and – oi, we're at Balaclava, best be gettin' off.'

'Wait! I forgot, we don't have tickets!'

'Yeah, well yer forgot about bein' with Barry the Bag, too.'

Having got off the train at Balaclava, Daniel pedalled the bicycle while Barry rode in the delivery basket. Soon they were at the edge of Acland Street. Barry hid the bicycle in the bushes of somebody's front yard, then they set off in search of anyone looking artistic and speaking with a foreign accent. They were trying to look as if they were freelance vendors of photographic artwork at a loose end, but in fact they resembled nothing more than a pair of schoolboys up to no good. On the other hand, this made them blend in perfectly, so there was no harm done.

After trying three cafés and discovering nothing more sinister than two Italians who did not speak English, they decided to loiter out on the street for a while. Barry nudged a discarded tobacco tin with his foot, then picked it up.

'Are you looking for secret messages from spies?' asked Daniel breathlessly.

Barry shook his head, then took another tin from his spare bag and emptied the few shreds of tobacco from the discarded tin into his own.

'Not enough baccy to make a fag, but it all adds up,' said Barry, holding out his own tin for Daniel to inspect. 'When this lot is full, I can sell it for seven pence.'

'*Arkoola*,' Daniel read on the side of Barry's tin. '*Kangaroo Fat Oil for the Relief of Haemorrhoids*.'

'I sells it to old McKenzie, the ganger. He thinks it's special, rare baccy from South America, and that I'm sellin' it cheap 'cause I stole it.'

'But surely one glance at the label —'

'Silly old bugger can't read,' said Barry suavely.

'We are supposed to be spies!' insisted Daniel, who was beginning to feel annoyed by Barry's attitude. 'We should be spying.'

'Jeez, Danny Boy, don't you know nothin'? Spies aren't folk wot go poncin' about in cloaks an' wavin' daggers. They blend in with the crowd, they look 'armless.'

'How would you know? Ever been a spy?'

'I done me share.'

'I don't believe you.'

'It's true! In the railways, you know. Stuff gets 'alf-inched, an', well, at the station I stands around, sweepin' and lookin' thick as two short planks tied together, so I hears stuff.'

'Stuff?'

'You know, coves talkin' about packages missin' and bein' hid in places. Soon as nobody's lookin', snap! It's in Barry's bag.'

'So you take it to the police?'

'Nah, I makes the contents available to folk of discernin' taste at reduced rates.'

'You *steal* from *thieves*?' exclaimed Daniel.

'Shush! Keep yer friggin' voice down!'

'Barry, two wrongs don't make a right.'

'Nah, but they makes a profit, and yer conscience don't kick up. Now then, keep an eye sharp for fag ends and baccy tins, and folk will think that's what we're doin'.'

'If Mother ever finds out about this, I'll never hear the end of it.'

Barry and Daniel decided to check the cafés again, sidling into them to check the floors for un-spent matches, partly smoked cigarettes, and even the occasional coin. As people got up to leave the tables, Barry finished off the discarded coffee in their cups. At the ninth café, Barry sat down at a table and actually ordered two coffees.

'You said we were supposed to blend in,' hissed Daniel.

'We are,' replied Barry. 'We're pretendin' to be customers.'

'But Mother says coffee is sinful.'

'Bullshit. Now then, what's the tally?'

Daniel produced a filing card and the stub of a pencil. He looked around. One of the girls across the room looked familiar, but he could not quite place her. She had long, flame-red hair ... and she suddenly turned to look straight at him! Daniel cringed down until his nose was almost touching the table as he recognised her as one of his sister's classmates from some school family day months ago. Daniel dragged his mind back to more global problems, and began to write.

'Out of nine coffee shops and cafés, three groups of people were speaking French, one was speaking Italian, and another was speaking Dutch.'

'Sounded like German to me.'

'I study this sort of thing at school, remember?'

'Yeah, yeah, each accordin' what 'e knows an' all.'

'In short, no Germans.'

'Next we'll – there's a copper on that table, off to yer right.'

'Where?' gasped Daniel, glancing around at once.

A man in a shabby suit gave a slight smile in their direction, then waggled his finger from side to side. Barry spread his hands and shrugged.

'He is not a policeman!' snorted Daniel, turning back to Barry. 'He has no uniform.'

'Nah, he's a copper spy. Constable, like.'

'The police have spies?'

'Yeah! Gotta be pretty stupid to be caught by one, mind, but there's some folk wot's that thick. Old Barrington there, like, 'e stops me an' searches me bag, last month. Finds a florin, an' says where did I steal it, like? I says please sir, I never done nothin', an' that I found it in the gutter. Old tosser keeps the florin an' lets me go with a caution.'

'But why not hide the florin too?'

'To give the twerp somethin' to find! Jeez, Danny Boy, don't you know nothin'? That made the cove pleased with 'imself, so he calls off the search of Barry's bag. Meantime, I has fifteen shillings in me secret bag bottom, and I now know what one more copper spy looks like.'

'So the florin was a decoy.'

'Yeah, sort of.'

Daniel was very well educated and was not short of intelligence, but Barry's sheer rat cunning had him awe-struck. Their two cups of coffee arrived, and while Daniel managed to force himself to drink his, he could not pretend to enjoy it. Patrons came and went. Daniel noticed that the girl with red hair kept staring at him. Muriel someone, that was her name. She and Emily did not like each other.

'Barry, there's a girl with a sketchbook over in the

corner, to my right. Long, red hair.'

'She's 'armless,' said Barry after flicking a glance across her.

'Is her name Muriel?'

'Yeah. Muriel Barker or Banker or somethin'.'

'Baker?'

'That's it! Her mum's got a shop, sells art stuff, an' she does stuff in some art school, too. Don't mind 'er. She's not police, she's not German, an' she's not sellin' nothin'.'

Barry began to break open his collection of discarded cigarettes and salvage the tobacco. Constable Barrington had five cups of coffee over the following half-hour.

'I can't see how he can drink so much,' muttered Daniel.

'Well, just watch – not right at 'im! Don't you know nothin'? Be casual, like. There, see, 'e added a bit of the old Lady Frisky to the cup.'

'Lady Frisky?'

'Whisky! From that silver flask.'

'Oh.'

'Reckon I could get a pound for that from Lurker the Worker. A guinea, if it was full.'

They sat there for another ten minutes, watching people come and go. From time to time men would come up to the plain-clothes policeman, and some would slip things into his hand. Daniel began to get used to watching people out of the corner of his eye.

He watched Muriel Baker a great deal. Although she was about the same age as Emily, Muriel dressed rather more exotically than Daniel's sister, and actually wore make-up. Her mother was something to do with the local artistic community. Barry had mentioned that. Daniel found himself thinking that Muriel was rather attractive, but he hurriedly reminded himself that she was as much as two years older than him. He was so intent on watching Muriel without being seen to watch her that he suddenly realised that he had missed a very important detail amid the noise, smoke and melodeon music in the café.

'The five men at that table beside Constable Barrington,' said Daniel softly, leaning across the table and looking directly at Barry. 'They're speaking German.'

'Yeah? Five Germans, and Foxy say that five Germans done the damage wot hasn't happened yet. Reckon we got them spies by the danglers, Danny Boy.'

It was at this point that Barry did the unthinkable. In his haste to dash off and speak to someone, he abandoned his bag to Daniel's care. Daniel laid a protective hand over the bag. Constable Barrington flicked a glance his way, but did not move. Within a minute Barry was back, having realised that he had parted company with his bag. He snatched it away from Daniel without a word, then embraced it for a moment, as if trying to make up to a jilted sweet-heart.

'Got the word on 'em,' Barry reported quietly. 'Waiter back there is Luker the Lurker.'

'Who is he?'

'Mate of Lurker the Worker, wot's a mate of Dad's on the railways. The German coves turned up three months ago. All speak English with accents when they want to order, and reckon they're artists. Can ya tell what they're saying?'

'Something about Australian wines being good, but that they would be much better if Germans made them.'

'Is that right, eh? Reckon that daft BC cove was talkin' chapter and verse?'

'Something about them just does not add up,' continued Daniel.

'Yeah? You spotted somethin'?'

'Well, their German is good.'

'What? Danny Boy, have a brain, they're Germans! Germans speak German better than anyone else.'

'No, not quite. I speak good English, but I don't speak it like an English teacher. Those five speak German like my German teacher. He always speaks German perfectly, so that his pupils don't get bad habits. Trust me, Barry, their German really is too good.'

'Don't see how that helps us.'

'Neither do I, but it's worth remembering.'

'Reckon we oughta get goin' now.'

'Why?' asked Daniel, casting a hurried glance at Muriel, who was still sitting by herself and occasionally sketching something on a pad. 'We just found the spies.'

'Yeah, but old Barrington is lookin' for 'is silver flask, an' I don't want to be in 'ere when the fun starts.'

'You couldn't have stolen his whisky flask, you never went anywhere near him.'

'Yeah, but Luker the Lurker did, then didn't I just go over to whisper with Luker the Lurker?'

'So you stole from the waiter what the waiter stole from the policeman?'

'Er, yeah. I sorta reckon stolen stuff is lost property, an' finders keepers is the rule there.'

Back in the street again, Daniel stood in front of Barry as he huddled in the doorway of a closed shop and hid the silver flask in the false bottom of his bag. Presently there were raised voices from within the café, and some minutes later Constable Barrington stormed out. Catching sight of Barry and Daniel, he strode over, seized Barry by the collar, and made him empty his pockets and open his bag. Finding nothing, he turned on Daniel, searched his pockets, and confiscated two shillings and a postcard.

'I'm watching you, sonny,' he said to Daniel as he turned to go.

Barry slapped Daniel reassuringly on the back as

Constable Barrington vanished into the crowd.

'He said he's watching me,' quavered Daniel.

'Yeah, so?'

'What if Mother finds out?'

'Jeez, Danny Boy, the cove says that to everyone. Is 'e watchin' ya now?'

'No, but –'

'Then there ya go!'

Barry and Daniel loitered outside the café. Muriel Baker came out, paused to glance at Daniel as if to confirm that he was who she suspected, then walked on. She's going to tell someone, thought Daniel. At least it won't matter if she tells Emily. Moments later Barry sampled the whisky from the stolen flask, and very nearly choked. It was while Barry was bent over with Daniel thumping his back that the Germans emerged from the café. With Barry gasping for air, they shadowed the group as they wandered along Acland Street, then turned down an alley. Telling Daniel to stay and watch, Barry dashed to another laneway to flank the Germans, but soon emerged looking angry and puzzled.

'Lost 'em!' muttered Barry. 'Did they come back out this way?'

'No. There were a lot of people coming and going, but nobody that looked like them.'

'Yeah? Then they either got some doorway to duck in, else they got disguises.'

A large, black coach rumbled out of the lane and

passed them. It was certainly not the sort of coach
that five artists could have afforded.

'Still, we know they're in town.'

'But wot else d'we know?'

'They are acting suspiciously. They speak German
too well, and they vanish after coffee.'

'Yeah, well, I bet your German teacher vanishes
into the dunny after he has a coffee, but that doesn't
mean we can nail him for tryin' to blow up parlyment. We lost 'em! Cove's a real worry if Barry the
Bag loses 'im.'

Daniel was ready to fall asleep as he and Barry
boarded a train going south at Balaclava Station, yet
Daniel knew that he still had to survive a dinner with
his family, Fox, and BC.

'Barry, do you, like, do that sort of thing all the
time?' he asked as the train pulled away from the
platform.

'Do wot?'

'Dodge the police, lurk about in cafés with artists
and secret police spies, all of that.'

'Nah, I just breezes in, nicks wot's easy, then comes
back in a month or two, when folks 'ave forgotten
me.'

'It was terrifying at the time, but now it seems so
exciting.'

'Excitin'? Wouldn't say that. It's business, ya know?

Dangerous business, but once ya got the rules, still business.'

'I felt like a master criminal.'

'Trust me, Dan the Man, we're just small-time thugs. Still, nobody bothers with the small fella, that's why I get by.'

'What did you think of Muriel?'

'The daft baggage in the café who was lookin' at ya?'

'Yes.'

'I'm not too popular with 'er mum. She wouldn't stock certain merchandise of mine in 'er shop.'

'Do you think Muriel's pretty?'

'Pretty?' responded Barry, as if he had once heard the word long ago, but it had not been explained to him.

'Yes, pretty. I think she is,' Daniel said dreamily.

'Yeah, so wot?'

'Nothing.'

It was clear to Daniel that in spite of all Barry's postcards, rubber devices, and luridly instructive books, the idea of romance had somehow bypassed him completely. Why does she have to be older than me? wondered Daniel, who thought of everyone who was both older than himself and female as a cross between a sergeant major and Emily.

They got off at North Brighton, where Barry's father shouted at him for not cleaning up the station for the following day's inspection. BC was gone from the packages room when Barry and Daniel checked there.

'Well, Dan, I got a cartload of work to get the place inspectional,' said Barry, taking a broom. 'Ya best be off to dinner.'

Daniel reached out for the broom. 'I'll sweep the platforms, Barry, you do the cleaning things that I don't know about.'

'Ya daft?' exclaimed Barry, who was clearly incredulous. 'Why?'

'I'll just be another bum on a seat at dinner, no harm done if I walk in late.'

'Ya still 'aven't said why.'

'You need help, and we're mates.'

Barry removed his grubby cap and scratched his greasy hair.

'Er, shit, ta. I mean, I got lots o' mates, but none wot would do nothin' for me. Not unless there was somethin' in it for them, anyways.'

'So, I'll sweep the platforms?'

'Yeah, yeah, but just sweep the dust onter the tracks as ya go, no big piles, inspectors don't like that. Oh, and toss the papers an' food scraps in a bin. Inspectors go on about encouragin' rats if ya sweep that stuff onter the tracks. I'll get the packages back in order in here, and give the place a dust. Lor, but

I 'ope yer sister can scav a room for that BC. He's a dark one an' I want 'im outta here. Wouldn't put it past 'im to shoot the bloody station inspector, judgin' from what he an' Foxy did to the push an' those three coppers.'

Daniel began to sweep. Part of what he had said to Barry was true. He did want to help his friend, but that was not the only reason that he was putting off his return home. For the past two hours or so he had been free and independent, taking chances and dodging danger. He wanted to wallow in the memory of being free of Emily and his mother, and of being heroic. Daniel had not only been useful, he had been indispensable. Alone, Barry would have been useless in Acland Street, even though he knew how to survive. Daniel could speak German and French, however, and at least identify a few other languages.

Alone with his thoughts, Daniel began to daydream about what was still to come. They were against hard, deadly men, men who would kill without hesitation, men who intended to murder thousands of innocent people. Daniel could not fight, and could not lead, but he wanted to be heroic. He was not even being given a chance to fight. Even Emily had been given a gun, but he had not.

Still, you don't have to be a leader or know how to fight to save the day, Daniel suddenly concluded. He imagined himself on the roof of the Exhibition Buildings, keeping watch as BC pulled a smoking fuse out of a huge, black bomb. Dead bodies lay everywhere. Suddenly the last German appeared with a gun. Daniel threw himself between BC and the German just as he fired, giving his life to save BC. Then Fox ran up and shot the German. As Daniel lay dying and BC thanked him for saving his life and saving the future, Emily arrived. She knelt beside him, started weeping hysterically and saying what a hero he was. Last words, must get the last words right, thought Daniel. How to get at Emily with my dying words? I did it for the Empire? No, too many dying heroes said that. I did it to save BC? No, boys did not say that about each other, even if it was true. Go away, let me die in peace? Yes! Perfect! With luck Emily would not even think of a reply before he was dead.

'Dan, mate, platform's lookin' good,' said Barry, coming up behind him.

'Go away, let me die in peace.'

'Yeah, feelin' a bit queasy meself. Reckon the milk was off in Luker the Lurker's coffee.'

'No, no! Sorry, I didn't mean … I mean … I meant, er, I was just rehearsing for a school play.'

'Yeah? Which one?'

'Macbeth,' replied Daniel, pulling the title out of his memory without really thinking about it.

'Yeah? Weren't he the Roman cove wot loved three

witches, but killed 'imself 'cause his father wouldn't let 'im marry —'

'Barry, take my advice and stick to petty theft.'

Daniel set off for home, this time with his thoughts on Muriel. He was, of course, younger than her, but she was very pretty. A pretty girl had stared at him. It was a pity that she was staring at him in order to be sure that he was Emily's brother doing something scandalous, like drinking coffee in a bohemian café. Was she worth dying for? Daniel imagined himself lying on the ground after being shot while saving BC and parliament. Muriel was cradling his head on her lap. Suddenly Daniel decided that it might be worth spending an hour or so dying. She might even kiss him. Perhaps he might even linger for a whole day. Daniel walked straight into a lamppost.

5

GENTLEMAN

Emily sat on her bed, staring unhappily at her doll collection. By now the dolls seemed vaguely ridiculous reminders of someone she had been a very long time ago, even though that time was only a day or two in the past. It was one thing to idolise an incredible hero in an image, but helping a real one was all too intense. Emily's fantasies of meeting BC involved introducing the brave and deadly warrior to her mother, having afternoon tea, and perhaps going to a ball together in a carriage. Now her hero was certainly going to meet her mother, but in a way that she had never dreamt. They had decided that his name would be Liore Besay, which was enough like Liore-BC so that nobody would ask questions if anyone used his real name.

'Greatness has been thrust upon me, and it is annoyingly heavy,' Emily announced to her dolls, but they remained silent.

Emily glanced at the coach clock on her dressing table. Her mother would be home in an hour, and soon after that Fox would arrive with BC. Emily wondered how she would survive the wait. Books! Now another memory called for her attention. Her brother had borrowed some issues of *Pearson's Magazine* from their father some months earlier, and Emily had in turn borrowed them from Daniel. They contained a serialised novel, *The War of the Worlds* by HG Wells. It was a tale of terrible octopus-shaped things from Mars invading England, and Emily had had nightmares about it for weeks afterwards. Although Daniel told her that Wells had also written a short novel about time travel, Emily had no interest in reading anything else by the author ... yet now the whole of her universe depended upon the feasibility of time travel. She padded quietly into Daniel's room and bent over before his bookcase. A check of Daniel's science books yielded nothing about time travel, or about Martians.

'Trapped, trapped, trapped!' she muttered as she paced the floor of her bedroom. 'I can order Daniel to go looking for German spies, but I can't even get a proper book. If I were a boy I could go straight down to the library to find whatever I wanted, but the librarian would tell Mother. Not fair, it's just not fair!'

Emily fought down the wave of frustration, resolving to take it out on Daniel for being a boy. Meantime it was clear that novels were the only source of information on time travel, so HG Wells was going to be her only hope.

Emily crept downstairs to her father's study, un-locked it with the spare key that Mr Lang thought he had lost, and scanned the authors and titles in his bookcases. The bookcase to the left of his desk con-tained the fiction, and she quickly located the books by authors whose names began with **W**. *The Time Machine: An Invention* turned out to be quite a slim volume compared to the other novels, but it was by HG Wells, so it had to be the right one. Back in her own room, Emily was relieved to find that Wells had included a short but plausible passage on the theory of time travel at the start of the story. This was the part that Daniel had said he found boring, but for Emily it was like digging up a trunk crammed with gold coins and jewels. Someone important enough to write books had said that time travel was possible, so it had to be true. She made notes as she read. By the time she had finished, her mother had arrived home. By now Emily was convinced that time travel was indeed possible, and that BC and Fox were definitely from the future. It was the work of moments to return the book to her father's study, then she went off to attend her domestic duties.

It was Mrs Lang's theory that Emily should spend some time in the kitchen every day, in order to become familiar with domestic matters and so be able to order servants about. Thus it was that Emily was standing by the stove, stirring the soup, when Fox and BC arrived. She heard the cast iron clapper of the front door rapping, then the sound of voices. They are big boys, they can take care of themselves, Emily reminded herself as she resisted the temptation to rush out and help them.

Suddenly Martha bustled into the kitchen carrying a tray and looking seriously worried.

'Oh Miss, oh Miss, nobody told me 'e was comin', and 'ere's me lettin' the 'ouse get in such a state!' babbled the maid to Emily.

'Who do you mean?' asked Emily, thinking at once that one of her father's important friends from the Melbourne Club had arrived unexpectedly.

'Young Lieutenant Liore, the officer from Master Fox's ship. I just comes in from the laundry ter lay the table, an' there 'e was, cheeks white like bone china, an' that scar from fightin' the mutineers, so brave, so 'andsome, like, an', oh Miss, what could 'e be thinkin' of me, lettin' the 'ouse look like this?'

Emily had forgotten that BC was actually very handsome and charismatic. Apparently he was also able to display great personal charm and perfect manners if necessary. Now that she thought about it, BC had everything that allured women without any of the qualities that repelled them. Emily arranged drinks on a tray while Martha frantically brushed and re-pinned her hair. Must remember to call him Liore, not BC, thought Emily as she entered the parlour.

BC was dressed in Fox's coat, but wearing it with a sense of style that Fox never could have managed.

'Ah, Emily, splendid,' said Mrs Lang. 'Lieutenant Besay, may I introduce my daughter Emily? Emily, this is Lieutenant Liore Besay, from Fox's ship.'

'Enchanted, Miss,' declared BC, who then bowed, took Emily's hand, and kissed it.

Emily shivered at the touch of his lips on her hand, but what was really impressing her now was that BC was acting like a true aristocrat, absolutely confident in himself, strangely graceful in every movement, good at putting people at ease, yet just slightly aloof and distant. Mrs Lang was not quite so flustered as Martha, but she was nervously wringing her hands.

'There was a terrible mutiny on the ship,' she explained to Emily in an unusually high voice. 'The authorities do not want word of it to be voiced around, in case other sailors get ideas.'

Fox had managed to clean, scrub and groom BC in the railway station's washroom, and between them they had put together a single, relatively undamaged uniform. Apart from the scar beside his right eye, BC's skin was now white and flawless, and his eyes so deeply green that they seemed almost black. He walked with an odd, wary elegance, and Emily fancied that he seemed like some prince visiting a servant's cottage. There was also something vaguely disturbing about him, however. Somehow he reminded Emily of a cat that had just finished its dinner, then found itself alone with the family parrot. For now he was harmless, but under different circumstances …

It was now that Mr Lang came in. He was introduced to BC, and was not sufficiently quick to deduce that any officer with a battle scar could quite probably be a strong, accomplished warrior. Concluding that the lean, pale, and almost beautiful youth needed to be shown that hale, clean living British people were strong, Mr Lang grasped BC's hand and squeezed hard as he shook. BC squeezed back. There was a crackling sound as various bones in Mr Lang's hand were ground against each other. He drew breath in a loud gasp, but managed not to cry out with the pain.

'Your pardon Sir,' said BC, putting a slight tinge of concern into his voice. 'I was told that in this country it is polite to squeeze back when shaking hands.'

'Quite all right,' wheezed Mr Lang, pressing his hand under his armpit. 'I've gone a bit soft, what with years of office work.'

Daniel appeared at this point. He announced to his parents that he had been upstairs and doing his homework, but they paid him no attention. He quickly took Emily aside.

'We found some Germans,' he whispered to Emily. 'Five of them.'

'Good, tell me later,' she whispered back.

BC displayed meticulous manners as dinner was served, and proved to be a master of polite conversation. Emily's parents found themselves flattered by the youth, yet they were desperate to please him. The talk meandered through no more than general banter and pleasantries, but finally BC seemed to decide that they could be allowed to discuss his background.

'I must leave early tonight, I have not been well,' he announced as the dinner plates were being cleared away by Martha – who had by now managed to change her dress, powder her face, and bind her hair up into another style.

'I can imagine, Lieutenant,' remarked Mr Lang. 'That's a nasty cut beside your eye. Seen action recently?'

'Indeed I have, Sir, I was in a mutiny,' replied BC.

'Oh capital! I bet the fellow who did that to you is feeling even more sorry for himself.'

'I doubt it, Sir, I killed him,' said BC softly.

There was complete silence for some moments.

'I – oh,' was as much as Mr Lang could manage at first, then he added, 'you were in the thick of it, then?'

'Indeed I was, Sir. I killed five before I was shot in the stomach.'

There was another lengthy and excruciatingly awkward pause. Even Emily had not known the full extent of the action when BC's unit had mutinied. It was Mrs Lang who took BC's bait.

'But Lieutenant, er, Liore – you don't mind me calling you Liore, do you?'

'You may indeed, ma'am.'

'Liore, the scar beside your eye is very fresh.'

'Indeed, ma'am, that is why I stayed in Melbourne, the action was quite recent. The wound to my stomach was so serious that I needed to spend some weeks ashore, recovering. I am staying in a rooming house at —'

'A *rooming* house?' boomed Mrs Lang, surging to her feet and flinging all thoughts of manners and dining room protocols to the winds. 'Oh no, no, no, no, that will never do! Martha? *Martha*!'

'Ma'am?' called Martha from just around the door, where she had been hiding to listen in.

'Martha, make up the bed in the spare room, the garret. Do it now! Lieutenant Liore will be staying here until he recovers his strength.'

'But —' began BC.

'Oh good, Liore, I knew you would agree. Ah, what did you say your title is?'

'Just lieutenant, ma'am,' replied BC with studied innocence. 'I am the youngest of my family, I did not inherit the title.'

'Oh my God, nobility, I knew it,' whispered Mrs Lang to her husband before bustling out of the door with Martha. Mr Lang was close behind them.

Emily, BC, Daniel, and Fox exchanged glances.

'Just as I said,' declared Emily smugly. 'Speak a few words in good English, dress in a neat uniform, display charm and good manners, and Mother will assume you are some earl's son. Now you will not be able to fight your way out of this house with a cutlass.'

'Near collapse, I am,' said BC, reverting to battle standard. 'Benzothoractine, effective, another half hour. Then, no more.'

'Good, very good,' said Emily. 'Stand up, take my arm, you must go and lie down on the sofa. Fox, kneel beside him. BC – Liore – unbutton your coat, and, um, could you please pull your shirt out to, ah, expose the bandage on your tummy?'

'Tummy?' asked Fox.

'Endearment term, archaic, stomach, for describing,' explained BC.

Emily stole a glance at BC's midriff. There was a patch of dried blood visible on the bandage.

'Fox, stay with BC. Whatever I do, stay with BC. Understand?'

'Lockdown.'

Emily drew breath, screamed, then dashed for the door. She collided with her father in the passageway.

'It's Liore, he's collapsed!' Emily shrieked.

Several minutes of chaos followed, but the bandages and blood established for the Langs by their own eyes that BC had indeed been shot in the stomach.

'My apologies, I stood up too quickly and became dizzy,' explained BC as Emily held his hand, Mrs Lang sponged his forehead, Mr Lang removed his boots, Daniel fanned him with a newspaper and

Martha stood ready with the smelling salts.

'With a wound like that, Sir, you should have stayed in bed for another month!' declared Mr Lang.

'Fox spoke well of you,' BC explained. 'You seemed to be fine people, and I was getting bored with lying in bed. I forgot how much blood I had lost, so when I tried to stand I could not –'

'You will go *straight* to bed, *now*!' ordered Mrs Lang. 'If I see you downstairs again before a week is past, I will *not* be at all happy.'

'Fox, BC, carry, upstairs,' said Emily quietly.

Fox lifted BC from the sofa as if he weighed no more than a feather-down pillow, and Daniel led the way upstairs with the entire family following. Presently BC was resting in the bed in the garret, and the cushions from the sofa had been put on the floor so that Fox could sleep beside him. With BC safely in bed, the Lang family gathered in the dining room.

'Your father and I think that you should, well, attend the young lieutenant,' Mrs Lang announced to Emily.

'Attend him?' asked Emily, batting her eyelashes at her mother.

'Don't you play coy with me, young lady!' snapped Mrs Lang.

'You know, sit by the bed, sponge his forehead, just be with him for an hour or two until he is settled,' interjected Mr Lang.

'I think you made a big impression on him,' her mother added smugly.

'Mother! We merely sat together at dinner.'

'Indeed so, but he has been at sea for a long time,' said Mr Lang. 'You are the first girl of, well, good breeding that he has met since coming ashore.'

'You never know,' added Mrs Lang.

'Need a chaperone?' asked Daniel, grinning slyly.

Fox had been left to look after BC, and the door to the garret was open as Emily reached it. Fox was lying on the cushions beside the bed, staring up at the ceiling and singing softly to himself.

> When first I deserted I thought myself free,
> Till my cruel parents informed on me.
> I was quickly followed after and brought back
>   with speed,
> And now the king's duty lies heavy on me.
> Court martial, court martial
> They very soon gave me,
> And the sentence I got
> Was three hundred and three.
>
> May the Lord have mercy on their souls
> For their sad cruelty
> For now the king's duty
> Lies heavy on me.

Emily knocked on the frame of the door.

Fox stopped singing. 'DBC, enter,' he said quietly.

'Please, do not stop,' said Emily.

'Unsuitable song, for polite girl, hearing.'

'Fox, I may be silly and sheltered, but I don't need protecting from soldiers' songs and stories.'

'Of shame, is song.'

'I did not know that deserters had their own songs.'

'People sing, of circumstances, for to bear.'

'Is that why you sing about a deserter? Because you attacked your own people in the future?'

'Of treason, songs, are none.'

'Well, yes, I suppose you did more than just desert. Do you regret what you did?'

'No. Leaders, courtly, all mad. Destroying world, for victory. Against courtly, we stand. Against Germans, we stand. Against world, we stand. Alone, we stand.'

'Yes, yes, and it is very brave of you, but now I have joined you, and Daniel, and Barry. I … I cannot say that I am truly happy, I must admit. I feel as if one of those gangs of men who used to kidnap people to serve aboard ships has captured me, and that I have been whisked away to sea.'

'Press-gang,' said Fox.

'Pardon?'

'Press-gang, sailors, abducted, crewing ships, for purpose of,' explained Fox in his terse but highly concentrated speech. He began to sing.

> As I walked out on London's streets
> A press-gang there I chanced for to meet
> They ask me if I would join the fleet
> Aboard of a man-o'-war, boys.'
>
> Come brother shipmates, tell me true
> What kind of treatment they give you.
> That I should know before I go
> Aboard of a man-o'-war, boys.
>
> When I got there to my surprise
> All that they told me were dirty lies.
> There was a row, and a jolly old row
> Aboard of a man-o'-war boys.
>
> The next thing they did, they took me in hand
> They lashed me with a tarry strand
> They lashed me till I could hardly stand
> Aboard of a man-o'-war, boys.

'Is more, as like,' said Fox. 'To Daniel, am teaching.'

'Strange, but you are right about singing and songs, they do make things easier to bear,' said Emily. 'Tell me, though, how can you sing in courtly, yet be so shy about speaking courtly?'

Fox looked uneasy, and did not reply immediately. Emily had the feeling that she had touched on a sensitive matter.

'Some songs, in courtly, may sing. *British Grenadiers, Heart of Oak, Rule Britannia, God Save the King.* Singing others, insolence, is considered.'

'Insolence?' gasped Emily. 'A song?'

'On target.'

Suddenly Emily remembered why she was there.

'My parents want me to sit with BC, and to sponge his forehead.'

'Why?'

'Because girls do that with wounded heroes.'

'No purpose, medical, is served.'

'Probably not, but it is very romantic.'

'No target.'

Emily had been fairly sure that romance would be well beyond Fox's experience.

'Romantic, you know. When boys and girls like each other. Grown-ups do it too, I suppose.'

'No target.'

'Romance is what they have before they are married.'

'No target.'

'Marry! What your parents did.'

'Mother, father, hatchery contract, signed. Marriage, for courtly, only.'

Emily suddenly felt so sad that she very nearly surrendered to tears. Only the fear of showing weakness in the same room as BC, even though he was unconscious, held her in check.

'Oh Fox, what a cruel, bleak world you come

from,' she sighed, caressing BC's hair while trying to tell herself that she was just smoothing it back.

'Is why, must prevent.'

For a time Emily just patted her damp sponge against BC's forehead. Because the youth was back in the healing coma he was quite oblivious to her attentions, but Emily was happy to be doing anything that involved BC.

'I need to talk with you,' she announced to Fox. 'It's about the mission.'

'Yes?'

'Daniel reported back to me. He and Barry found five very suspicious Germans in St Kilda.'

'Target acquired. Orders?'

'Orders?'

'Abduct? Interrogate? Torture? Kill?'

'I can't tell anyone to do things like that!' exclaimed Emily, as her mind conjured the image of a German being stretched on a rack being operated by Barry the Bag, who was wearing a hood.

'DBC must.'

Suddenly Emily understood a lot more about Fox. He had been brought up to see everything as absolutely black and white, and to think of anything British as absolutely white.

When thought of in those terms, the fact that he had actually rebelled was almost beyond belief. Because he spoke only battle standard, he sounded as if he was somewhat slow of wit, yet under all that he was probably fiercely independent and highly intelligent. Now he needed something to cling to. His commander, BC, had been that. Now Emily was his commander.

What must he think of me? wondered Emily. I must look like a village idiot compared to BC. There was nothing for it, she just had to be honest.

'Just what am I expected to do?'

'Clarify, if please?'

'What do I do as DBC?'

'Lead.'

'But for how long? BC is very sick.'

'Is strong, will live.'

'Yes, but he is not going to be able to *do* anything for a long time. The opening of the first Australian parliament is very soon, and that is when the bombs go off, important people die, and the future changes.'

'Ninth day, May,' said Fox instantly.

'Thank you. So that means that if BC is still too weak to get up, I shall be leading you when we try to stop the bombers.'

'Estimate fifty-five per cent, adjusted deviation fifteen per cent.'

'Um, could you say that again in English, please?'

'BC lead, is possible, still. Is likely, you lead.'

Emily put a hand to her head. 'No wonder the bombers win,' she said wearily. 'Whatever shall I do? I can't fight, I can't lead, and if Mother had her way I would never leave the house without a chaperone.'

'So far, safe lodging, for BC, secured. Surveillance, in St Kilda, organised. Germans, in St Kilda, discovered. As leader, scoring wins. Myself, as leader, not capable.'

'But I do not know how to use a gun.'

'In Flinders Lane, did so.'

'Well yes, I suppose I pointed a gun to frighten some snotty boy, but I could never shoot someone.'

'Is hard, you think? Is easy. Too easy. Spare time, ten minutes, I teach.'

'Too easy? Fox, I sometimes think that you disapprove of guns.'

'On target.'

'Really? A soldier who does not like guns?'

'On target.'

'So what do you like?'

This was obviously a very sensitive matter. Fox clasped his hands together, then squeezed until the colour drained from beneath his fingernails.

'Art, my liking. Impressionists. Heidelberg School. Symbolists, also. Music, am liking. Dance music. In band, of playing, do dream.'

To Emily, this was like walking onto a warship and finding an art gallery and ballroom below the deck. Artistic people talked like artistic people. Talking to Fox was like meeting a guard dog whose hobby was collecting Ming Dynasty porcelain. Emily knew that she was trapped by her parents, but Fox was trapped by people who were not even born yet. They were deep within his mind, and Emily could not begin to imagine the conflicts that were going on there between artist and warrior.

She stared at BC, wondering what was within his head. He had been the leader of the finest of the Empire's finest cadets, he had everything, yet he had rebelled. His sheer strength of character must have been unimaginable. What did he like? Was he artistic, like Fox, or was he a warrior all the way through? Emily sponged BC's forehead and held his hand. His breathing remained deep and steady, his pulse slow.

'When will BC be fully recovered?' she asked as the grandfather clock downstairs chimed out 10pm.

'Operational, six weeks. Functional, seven days.'

'Seven days?' echoed Emily. 'But that means that he can take over from me before the opening of parliament.'

'Functional. Not optimal. Functional, fifty-five per cent probability. Adjusted deviation fifteen per cent.'

'But he could tell me what to do.'

'On target.'

'That is such a relief.'

'Seven days, much work, stop bombers, still must.'

'Stop the bombers? With me leading?' Emily laughed for the first time since the boating accident.

'On target.'

'If the future depends on me, then the future must indeed be fixed.'

'No target,' insisted Fox. 'Not fixed, is future.'

'Perhaps so, but I am becoming more and more certain that the future is very hard to change.'

'On target.'

'I should go to bed, there is nothing that I can do for BC. Nothing useful, anyway.'

'Beside bed, shall sleep,' announced Fox.

Emily returned to her room, stared at her little table for a moment, then rummaged in the drawers. In one book of art paper were several sketches of BC, but the rest of the paper was blank. Emily cut out the sketches and stared at them for a time. The likenesses were not bad, but after having sat beside BC, holding his hand, she was no longer quite so interested in clinging to sketches. She hid the sketches under her mattress, then picked up her pencils and charcoals. Returning to the garret, she found the door still open and Fox settling down for the night on the cushions beside the bed.

'Don't you ever lock doors?' asked Emily.

'Is forbidden, by provosts, of academy.'

'But Fox, this is a hundred years in your past. The Imperial War Academy is a school for boys, and there are no provosts. You can do what you like.'

'Cannot. Cadet training, is mine. Take away, is left, what?'

'You are trapped, just like I am trapped,' Emily concluded.

'Are trapped, yourself?' exclaimed Fox, sitting up quickly and looking for some possible threat.

'No, no, not the way you think. Just being a girl traps me.'

'No target.'

'Sorry, sorry, I just can't explain,' she said, giving up on the cultural gulf between them and holding out the sketch pad, charcoals and pencils instead. 'Fox, these are for you. Now you can do artwork. Sketches, anyway.'

'Plan, you have?' responded Fox, taking her offerings as if they were the British crown jewels.

'No, these are a present.'

'Present? Is what?'

He does not even understand what a present is, thought Emily, feeling too tired to fight her way through yet another explanation.

'Never mind. Look, with these you can go to the cafés in St Kilda, pretend to be an artist.'

'Artist? Me?' responded Fox, looking as if he had been asked to lower his trousers.

'Yes, you know, spy on people while you sketch.'

'Spy?' asked Fox hopefully, looking a little less alarmed.

'It is a disguise.'

'Camo!' exclaimed Fox, delighted. 'On target! Lockdown! Emily-DBC, good leader.'

Good leader, thought Emily. If only you knew. She paused at the door, then turned back.

'Why are you called Fox?' she asked. 'Do you mind me asking?'

'Distinct call-sign, no mistaking. Fox! Del! Jet! Bow! Even Dan! In battle, no confusing.'

'So even your names are for fighting?'

'On target.'

'But sad.'

Emily paid another visit to her father's study. Back in her room, she read the first few pages of HG Wells' story on time travel yet again, and made more notes. Several things worried her. If BC changed the future that had formed him, then he would cease to exist. That meant that he would never come back from that future. That in turn meant that the Exhibition Buildings would always be bombed. Emily concluded sadly that the future was indeed fixed, and that this little sliver of time where she was nursing BC back to health was doomed. In nine days BC and Fox would cease to exist – and would never have existed.

Yesterday will change, thought Emily. BC and Fox come here, then they cease to be. Daniel and I never get rescued by Fox. In a few days, if BC stops the bombing, I shall be over a week drowned, and the bombing will happen anyway. If BC fails, the dreadful century of war will happen anyway, yet BC and Fox will remain real.

For some minutes Emily sat waiting for her head to stop spinning, then got out of the chair, changed into her nightdress, took Barry's book on human sexual reproduction from under her mattress, and got into bed. This time she read certain sections with considerably more care than before. Hundreds of coyly worded scenes in dozens of romantic novels began to make sense as she read.

Sex was apparently the ultimate means to demonstrate one's love! There were certainly dangers from rather worrying diseases, and the threat of pregnancy loomed large over what Emily now understood seduction to mean, yet it remained the ultimate expression of love. In novels, girls did it with sweethearts about to go away to war. BC was already at war, and was about to face his final battle. Win or lose, he would die. They would all die – or vanish, or never exist, or whatever happened when one travelled through time and did things that changed things that had not happened yet but had happened anyway.

After hiding the book again, Emily blew out the lamp and lay stretched out in her bed. Her mother said that good girls always slept on their side, and that it was rude to lie flat on one's back. Emily thought of BC, and of how they would soon all be dead. Without even making a conscious decision, Emily slipped from her bed, removed her nightdress, then climbed into bed again and lay on her back. She did not sleep very much for the rest of the night, and when her mind was not on BC, she was planning what to do with his crew while he lay in the healing coma. That was not all that she was planning.

'Trap me, will you, Mother and Father?' she whispered into the darkness. 'Keep me out of libraries, and bohemian coffee houses, and, and even grocery stores? I lead a squad of killers! Well, apart from Daniel and Barry, anyway. I have a gun that can melt steel. I have been trusted to save the future! No, Mother and Father, you cannot stop me. You have ordered me about for the very last time.'

6

GIRLFRIEND

For Daniel the morning began normally enough. He awoke, washed, checked with Fox that BC was still alive, then went downstairs with Fox to breakfast. Mrs Lang had decided that everyone except for BC should eat breakfast in the dining room. Daniel entered the room, sat down, and gestured for Fox to do the same. Emily was already there, her fingers interlocked, her chin resting on them, and her elbows on the table. As far as Daniel could recall, nobody had ever put their elbows on a table in the Lang household, at least not in his short lifetime.

For some moments Daniel stared in fascination, then he looked up at Emily's face. Her expression told him that he should seriously consider feeling alarmed, or even consider the option of blind panic.

Martha was serving as well as cooking. She brought in a rack of hot toast, and Daniel served himself at once. His theory was that something unimaginably harrowing was about to happen, so that soon nobody would feel inclined to actually eat breakfast at the breakfast table. Daniel glanced at Emily whenever it seemed safe to do so. She was not eating. That was also a bad sign. Emily always ate, even when she was not hungry. She ate with manners so maniacally good that even her parents could not match them. Emily actually read books about manners, memorising lengthy passages and tormenting Daniel with them. Now her elbows were on the table. That was bad manners, and so it was a very bad sign.

Daniel was up to his fifth piece of toast and jam when Mr and Mrs Lang finally entered. They sat down, still discussing BC and whether or not a proper doctor should be summoned to examine him. This suddenly secured Fox's attention. He assumed the expression of a tiger that had been sleeping in the sun and had awoken to find two lambs playing with his tail.

'How shall I eat thee, let me count the ways,' mumbled Daniel to himself.

Nobody seemed to hear. Suddenly Mrs Lang finally noticed that her daughter had her elbows on the table.

'Emily, attend your manners!' called Mrs Lang in quite a sharp tone.

Emily let her interlocked hands fall to the table. She did not attempt to move her elbows back. This is it, she's going to take on Mother, thought Daniel. Why can't I get something easy to do, like getting shot while saving BC? Emily turned and glared down the table in the direction of Mrs Lang. Should one have a big breakfast on Judgement Day? Daniel toyed with the idea of having a sixth piece of toast. After all, it was not as if being hungry was going to be much of an issue with the world about to end.

'Liore needs a proper nurse, so I should have the rest of the week off school to look after him,' Emily announced. 'Mother, will you inform school?'

'Well, I …' began a very indignant Mrs Lang.

'Thank you,' said Emily brusquely before she could say anything else. 'Now Father, Fox has seen the police, and they have recovered the things that were stolen from him when he arrived in Melbourne.'

'Your pardon …' began Fox, apparently distracted from thoughts of killing anyone who tried to prevent him caring for BC.

Emily went straight on. 'That means that Fox has no need to work as a delivery boy for a grocer. He should be going to a mechanics institute and learning about electricity.'

'Oh, why yes, what good news,' managed Mr Lang, reeling from the barrage of orders from his daughter.

'Fox, notice, to Aitkinson, submit, this morning,' ordered Emily.

'Lockdown!' Fox barked back at once.

'But I could nurse the young lieutenant,' managed Mrs Lang, rallying slightly.

'Mother, you are busy with all the social engagements leading up to the opening of parliament,' Emily stated in a tone that was not to be argued with.

'But you will be alone with him!' exclaimed Mrs Lang, deciding to argue anyway.

'Martha and Henry will be in the house. Besides, Lieutenant Liore is honourable in the extreme, and he is recovering from a bullet wound to the stomach.' Daniel noted that Emily's eyes were huge and un-blinking, like those of a cat gathering itself to spring onto a bird. 'I am in no danger of being seduced.'

What followed was the longest five-second silence of Daniel's entire life. Emily had an odd talent of forcing people to do what they did not wish to, and now her utterly mortified brother realised how she did it. When Emily wanted something minor, and someone did not want to give it to her, she stepped out far beyond everyday, polite, conventional manners. Her victim then had the choice of touching off a major scene, or merely giving in to her for the sake of keeping the peace. Whether parting Barry from his bag at the point of a death ray, or saying something so unimaginably embarrassing to her parents that they would rather give her a week off school than discuss the matter further, Emily always won. Daniel tried to imagine Emily taking her clothes off and getting into BC's bed. Daniel's imagination screamed for mercy.

'Well, of course I trust you both,' babbled Mrs

Lang at last.

'Splendid, Mother, I just knew everyone would be mature and reasonable about this matter.'

'Now just a minute …' began Mr Lang, his face flushing red with anger.

'Besides, Father, you and Mother *were* content to leave me alone in the house with Henry, before I knew the meaning of the word seduce,' Emily continued smoothly. 'Oh, and I had to find out the meaning of the word for myself!'

The skin of Mr Lang's face faded to a deathly pallor, and his mouth hung open, unmoving. This cannot be happening, thought Daniel. My sister has taken on our parents, and she is winning.

'I am highly responsible about the temptations of the flesh, Father, even though you and Mother were too embarrassed to tell me about them,' Emily continued. 'Oh, and Daniel knows too, I thought it my duty to tell him.'

I do believe the truth has just been run down and trampled by a herd of stampeding elephants, thought Daniel, cringing so low that his chin began pressing into the sixth piece of toast, which lay cooling on his plate. On the other hand, I don't suppose that anyone wants to know that I really learned what bums, titties and dicks are for from Barry the Bag.

'Well then, ah, so you know how babies are made?' asked Mr Lang, staring at Daniel.

If I stabbed my hand with my fork, perhaps it

would distract people a little and they would change the subject, thought Daniel. Then again, perhaps they would not notice, and I would go through all that pain for nothing. Daniel flicked a glance at his father. Mr Lang was still staring at him. Well, the alternative is to stare at Emily, thought Daniel. I suppose he only needs to hear me say 'yes', Daniel was concluding when Emily came to his rescue.

'He also knows how they are *not* made, Father.'

Mr Lang suddenly assumed the expression of a small mouse confronted by a large cat in a very tight corner. Mrs Lang put a hand to her forehead and closed her eyes. Daniel tried unsuccessfully to sink through his toast, his plate, the table and the floor. Fox was aware of tension at the table, but was also aware that none of it was directed at him, and that Emily appeared to be mistress of the situation. Reassured that his commander was winning against superior odds, he continued eating his breakfast, perfectly at ease.

'Well then, everything is really under control,' Mr Lang said as he turned to the clock. 'Look at the time, I'm late already, must dash.'

'Wait, I have to go with you, remember?' called Mrs Lang, getting up so hastily that she knocked her chair over.

Daniel stood up as his mother left the table, and so did Fox. The piece of toast was stuck to Daniel's chin.

'Standing, are males, when females, leave table,' said Fox as they sat down again. 'Why?'

'Manners,' muttered Daniel, peeling the toast from his chin.

'Manners, teaching Fox? Yes?'

'Yes,' said Daniel listlessly.

Now Emily turned her gaze on Daniel, and she was smiling. That was bad, Daniel knew from experience.

'As you have just seen, brother dear, I do *not* need to be holding a death beam gun that can melt steel in order to force people to do what I want. I am going to give you back that, that *science* book about making babies, and Barry can have his bag back too. Bring him here after school. I have orders for both of you. Now go.'

'Babies, in hatchery, are made,' said Fox, looking puzzled.

'I have a book that I think you should read,' replied Emily.

Moments later Daniel was out of the door and hurrying for the sanctuary of the railway station.

Press-ganged, thought Daniel. I've been press-ganged into some army that does not even exist, and by my own sister. By the time he reached the station Daniel was singing the old song that he had learned from Fox.

Well the next thing they did,
They took me in hand,
They lashed me with a tarry strand.
They lashed me till I could hardly stand,
Aboard of a man-o'-war, boys.

'Thinkin' of runnin' away to sea, Danny Boy?' asked Barry, who was loitering by the station gate.

'Life at sea is starting to look good, even if I have to endure floggings and drink rum,' sighed Daniel.

'Problems at the big house?'

'Emily has … well, to cut a very embarrassing story short, she is even ordering our parents around. I never thought I would be so happy to go to school.'

'Any word on me bag?'

'She will be returning the bag and the book after school today. On the other hand, she expects us to continue spying on the Germans.'

'Yeah?'

'Yes. Sorry, but Emmy just has ways of making people do things.'

'Dunno if that's bad, I sorta fancy this stuff.'

'What do you mean? This is not an adventure book, Barry, those are real spies with real bombs – and guns, and daggers.'

'But it's important. Like, when me, Barry the Bag, was hanging about with ya sellin' French postcards, I wasn't just a dirty little cove sellin' French post-cards.'

'But Barry, you *were* a dirty little cove selling French postcards, and so was I. If my Mother ever finds out, bloody hell, don't even talk about it!'

'Danny Boy, ya don't understand. Yesterday I was a secret warrior of the British Empire, I was important! I'se never been important. I keep thinkin' that the king might give me a medal or somethin', you know, for bein' brave and loyal.'

'I would rather not get the medal than have my mother find out about yesterday.'

'Yeah, well, there ya go Danny Boy, but I'm different. One day yer old man will give ya lots of money and a job in 'is business, and yer'll have yer own carriage and house, and be important. I'll just be sellin' tikkies for the rest of me days, but now I can think back and say, oi, I helped the king once.'

'So what are you going to do?'

'Reckon I'll dodge school for the rest of the week, an' hang about, helpin'.'

'But you dodge school anyway.'

'Oi, that's yer train comin', Danny Boy. See ya, four hours past noon, an' all that toffy stuff?'

'Well, yes, I suppose.'

'Barry needs 'is proper bag, Danny Boy. Important spyin' equippyments in the bag.'

School dragged slowly for Daniel, even though it had the attraction of being time spent away from Emily.

Predictably, there was a great deal about Australian history in general and federation in particular. Daniel listened to his history teacher speculate on what would follow federation.

'Australia is destined to become the greatest nation in the Southern Hemisphere!' concluded the teacher. 'You boys are destined to become the leaders of the very finest nation in the British Empire of the future.'

If only you knew, thought Daniel morosely.

'And now, I want you all to write an essay on what Australia will be like a hundred years from today. Two hundred words, and you may go home once it is on my desk.'

Daniel contemplated writing an essay about death rays, bombs that could destroy entire cities, the space service, Britain occupied by Germany and Melbourne as the capital of the British Empire. Tempting, he thought, before scrawling out a scenario of Britain's industries transferred to Australia's deserts so that the English countryside did not have to be so spoiled by soot from factories. As essays went, it was not among his best, but given all that was on his mind, Daniel thought it quite a credible effort. At three-thirty he met with Barry at the North Brighton Station, and together they set off for an audience with his increasingly fearsome sister.

❈

Emily met with the two boys in her bedroom. She sat on her bed while they sat on the floor. On her table were the bag and the book. Cradled in her arms, as if it were a favourite doll, was BC's death ray weapon. Daniel noticed that one of her dolls looked suspiciously like BC.

'You may have those, those *objects* on the table,' Emily declared in a manner that was both regal and disapproving at the same time.

Barry surged up and enfolded his bag in his arms, then tossed the book to Daniel. Daniel slid the book under his shirt. Emily tossed a coin to Barry.

'What is that?' she demanded.

'Er, a shillin'.'

'On target. It is the king's shilling. Daniel, here is one for you. The pair of you have just taken the king's shilling, and are thus in his service. It is important to keep old traditions alive, and besides, we need some ceremony for something as important as joining the SYS-IK crew.'

Daniel examined his shilling. The monarch's profile was that of a man, and the name was Charles III. The date was 1997.

'Oi, there's some of me postcards missin'!' exclaimed Barry, who was by now rummaging in his bag.

'I have requisitioned five of your French postcards for use in the fight against those plotting to bomb the opening of parliament.'

'Wot, ya mean yer gonna change the future by mailin' dirty postcards to —'

'Trust me Barry, it's a really bad idea to talk back to an officer,' cautioned Daniel, 'especially when that officer is my sister.'

'The cards will be returned to you at the end of the mission, BarryS1. Now here are your orders. You will return to those bohemian cafés in St Kilda, the ones where the artists gather to drink coffee, and ...'

'Talk about bein' decadent!' volunteered Barry.

'What is decadent?' asked Emily.

'Er, sorta bein' rude, but proud of it.'

'Yes, well, I am sure you would know. Anyway, I sent FoxS3 there this morning, with a sketch pad.'

'I thought spies needed guns and daggers,' said Daniel, thinking it unfair that Emily had kept the death beam while it was Fox, Barry and himself who were facing danger.

'It's disguises, Danny Boy. It's what Foxy calls camo.'

'But, but surely if Fox had the death-beam gun he could shoot all the Germans at once, before the Exhibition Buildings are bombed.'

'That'd be murder!' exclaimed Barry.

'No it would not,' said Daniel. 'As far as Fox is concerned, the Germans are guilty of murder a hundred years in the future, but a hundred years ago – for him. I mean, they would deserve to be executed if they had not escaped and died of old age or something, so now they are still alive and intend to kill all those people, so they are already guilty of murder.'

Barry looked blank for a moment. 'Danny Boy, you lost me back at "no",' he confessed.

'You have forgotten one vital point,' said Emily. 'Just suppose there are more than those five Germans? The others will just be more careful.'

'We could tell the people who run things,' insisted Daniel.

'And who would believe five children?'

'We got a death beam,' Barry pointed out.

'Look, BarryS1, if we fronted up, told our story, then cut a tree down with one blast from this gun as proof, the gun would be locked away while the police tried to work out who we stole it from. Nobody takes children seriously!'

There was nothing in all of the world that Daniel disliked more than to agree with his sister, but on this occasion she did have a strong and valid argument.

'So what do we do?' he asked.

'We watch and wait. You and Barry will relieve Fox at the café, and he will go and scout around the Exhibition Buildings. Danny, be home by dinnertime, else Mother will worry. Barry, stay as long as you can.'

'On target, DBC!' said Barry smartly.

Emily shot a suspicious glance at Barry, as if she

suspected that he might be lampooning her authority. On the other hand, Daniel noticed that Barry
was not smiling, or even grinning.

'DBC, what if we have learned nothing useful by
the opening of parliament?' Daniel asked, now worried that his sister might have thoughts about leading
them into real combat.

'BC will be well enough to take over by then.'

'But what if he's not?'

'Then I have a plan, a very simple plan. I shall
be there, on the morning. Father plans to be in the
grounds with Mother and us two. He likes to be
present at important occasions. He says it is being
part of history.'

'So?'

'So if we have not yet uncovered the truth by
then, I shall shoot this death beam at trees and the
surrounding buildings, setting them afire and causing
lots of panic. The opening of parliament will be
cancelled, and everyone will be evacuated. I have
everything covered, you see? We cannot lose.'

By now Barry had gone very pale, and he sat rocking back and forth with his bag in his arms. Daniel
suddenly realised that he was sitting with his own
mouth hanging open. Deciding that there was very
little point in trying to reason with his obviously
manic sister, he said nothing.

'I have spent the afternoon reading about the
Duke of Wellington,' Emily continued.

''Ere, weren't he the cove wot told a woman wot he'd 'ad seductive relations with to publish an' be damned?'

Emily glared at Barry, but pointedly said nothing.

'Er, Barry, remember what I said about talking back to officers?' asked Daniel.

'Yeah, oh! Sorry, DBC, like.'

'If I may continue,' said Emily coldly, 'the Duke of Wellington beat Napoleon, so he was a very good soldier and leader. He used to tell his generals to try to think like he did, so that when they were amid the confusion of battle, and separated from him, they would anticipate what he would want them to do.'

'Wot's anticipate?' asked Barry.

'Know without being told,' muttered Daniel. 'In this context, anyway.'

'Here is my next order for you, DanS2 and BarryS1,' Emily concluded. 'In the days ahead, when you find yourselves cut off from me or BC, you are to look out for *any* means to stop the bombing. It does not matter what it is, just do it.'

Ten minutes later, Daniel and Barry were at North Brighton Station, waiting for a train with the station bicycle.

'I do believe my sister has gone dippy,' said Daniel unhappily.

'Dunno,' replied Barry. 'Like if BC 'ad said all

that, we'd be saying wot a good plan it was, and how brave and clever the cove is.'

'Barry, my sister has a gun that can sink a battleship. A really *big* battleship. Now she says she wants to use it when parliament's opening, just to frighten people.'

'So? I'd be frightened.'

'But don't you understand? She's a girl! Girls can't shoot. Father says that every time women come to the archery range. Emmy exploded an area of seawater the size of a football field with that death beam and still missed the buoy she was aiming at. If she tried to shoot a tree with that thing, well, she might kill more people than the bombers mean to! You saw what it did at the beach. The war with Germany might start anyway.'

'Nah, they'll just say it was some daft baggage with a death ray, and ...'

'And?' prompted Daniel.

Barry scratched his head. 'Yeah, well, maybe we do 'ave a problem.'

Once again the two boys arrived in Acland Street in the late afternoon and began their investigations. This time they knew who they were looking for, but they had new problems. The problems started with Luker the Lurker catching Barry and demanding that he return the silver hip flask that he had stolen. Barry returned the flask. Moments later Luker and Barry were confronted by Constable Barrington, backed up by two police in uniform. Barrington demanded the return of the very same flask, and of course it was found in the possession of Luker. Luker immediately accused Barry of planting it on him. Barry's defence was that he 'never done nothin'.'

Daniel managed to avoid the exchange – merely by not looking like the sorts of people that Barrington thought were criminals. Leaving Barry to his own devices, Daniel decided to keep a lookout for the Germans, wait for Fox, and avoid anyone else who might know him. With Barry unlikely to be any help for some time, Daniel bought a coffee and sat at a vacant table. Seldom have I ever felt quite so alone, he thought. No friends, nobody I could die for.

'*Bonjour, chérie*, may I join you at your table?'

The speaker was female, and about the same age as Emily, but a lot more stylishly dressed. She had long, flame-red hair which she wore only partly pinned. The word 'wanton' crossed Daniel's mind. The word 'Muriel' followed it very quickly.

'I, er, yes, do sit down,' said Daniel, wondering whether despair or exasperation would be the right emotion to feel.

'Were you waiting for a girl, or perhaps an artist friend?' asked Muriel.

'An artist, his name is Fox. Neat hair, broad shoulders, never smiles, carries a sketch pad.'

'I know him,' gasped Muriel, her deliberate French accent almost faltering. 'By him I am frightened. He sits in the cafés and sketches.'

'He's actually very shy and gentle.'

'Oh is he? Is that not the way of the world? Someone who looks so fierce and dangerous is really a gentleman, yet someone as innocent looking as you could be a terrible murderer.'

'Sorry, I'm just a schoolboy. My name is Daniel.'

'Ah, and let me introduce myself. I am Michelle, and I come from Paris.'

'Actually you're Muriel Baker from Balaclava. Your mother runs an art supply shop in Carlisle Street; you go to school with my sister, Emily, and if I were you I would go easy on that French accent before someone from France hears you and starts laughing.'

Daniel had not really intended to be quite so brutal, it was just that he treated everyone who was older than himself and female as a dangerous predator. The girl looked rather hunted for a moment, and began to glance about nervously.

'Um, are you going to tell anyone?' she asked, having satisfied herself that nobody else was within earshot.

'Don't be silly,' muttered Daniel. 'I'm nervous enough about being seen here myself.'

'Does Emily know?'

'Yes. She sent me here.'

Muriel's eyes bulged. 'She did?'

'Yes. Emily is a sort of master criminal,' explained Daniel with a feeling of malicious satisfaction. 'She stays at home most of the time, and makes other people go out and do things for her – and get into trouble.'

'My goodness! And here I was thinking that she was just a stuck-up, know-it-all prig.'

'She's that too,' said Daniel.

There was a pause as Muriel thought about everything that she had just learned about Emily and Daniel.

'I'm very artistic,' Muriel declared. 'I don't think Emily likes artists. In class she says that artists have loose morals.'

'Well, I like artists and I don't like Emily,' replied Daniel, without realising that he had just responded to an invitation to become rather special to Muriel.

Muriel smiled impishly, then squeezed Daniel's hand for a moment.

'I … I … I'm surprised your mother lets you come here,' he stammered while trying to come to terms with the idea of a girl holding his hand, even though he was not lying mortally wounded after having been shot defending her.

'Oh, Mother is very liberal. She closes the shop when I get home from school and we come here to-gether on our bicycles. She models for art students in a studio not far from here. I sit in cafés and meet peo-ple. The Heidelberg School artists come here. Isn't that exciting? A whole new style of Impressionist art named after somewhere in Melbourne.'

Daniel had seen artists painting at the local beach, but that was Brighton, not Heidelberg. Rather than make a fool of himself, he decided to change the subject.

'What does your father have to say about all this?'

'He died of typhoid when I was little.'

'Oh, I'm sorry.'

The chasm between Daniel's lifestyle and that of Muriel yawned wide and deep, suddenly robbing him of anything to say that was even halfway sensible. He did quite desperately want to say something sensible, because for the very first time a girl was taking an interest in him. Actually that was not entirely correct. Emily took an interest in him, in the same way as a wolf takes an interest in a lost chicken with clipped wings and a limp. Muriel's interest was making his heart pound, raising his temperature, and putting a tremor in his hands. At last Muriel took the initiative.

'I have only seen you here once before,' she said, clasping her hands in front of her.

'I've started coming here to meet my artist friend, Fox. He's, er, also doing things for Emily.'

'Oh. I wondered why other artists did not know him. I know lots of artists and writers. My mother takes me to Fasoli's in Lonsdale Street sometimes.'

'Fasoli's?'

'It's a very bohemian café. I have met Norman and Lionel Lindsay, and Fred McCubbin, Mr Nerli, and there are even women like Katherine Mansfield and Ruby … I can't remember her other name. Anyway, they are very, very clever people, and the talk is so inspiring. Mr Lindsay and Mr Nerli do pictures of orgies. Can you imagine that? They are people who are going to change the world.'

I know some people who are going to change the world, too, thought Daniel. Thing is, they are going to use something a bit stronger than poems and paintings.

'I want to be an artist, too,' Muriel continued. 'Mother supports the idea. She says that women are moving into all sorts of occupations where they could be better than men.'

'They are?'

'Yes. When we go to school, who does more art? Girls or boys?'

'Girls, I suppose.'

'Yes! And who are all the famous artists?'

'Well …'

'Men! Name me a single female artist.'

'Well …'

'See? You can't. More women do art than men, but then they are held back so that only men can be famous. I mean, you would pay my mother to model for you, but would you buy one of her paintings?'

Daniel tried to persuade his imagination to picture Muriel's mother with her clothes off. Daniel's imagination retreated to a room deep inside his head, slammed the door, and refused to come out.

'I, that is, wouldn't have the money to buy a painting,' he managed.

'Well, you know what I mean. I could get modelling work any time that I wanted it, but I always refuse. I want to be an artist, and nothing else is good enough.' Now she leaned across the table and whispered conspiratorially. 'Do you know why I came over to you?'

'I look harmless?' ventured Daniel.

'No, silly! You look young and fresh and exciting, unspoiled by all the notions that older men have got about girls not being able to do things.'

'Oh. Thank you,' replied the astounded Daniel.

'There are so few boys who like art. I despise boys who think they are little gods because they are good at football or cricket.'

'My sister just despises all boys, but she still uses them.'

'Your sister really has old-fashioned ideas. Women are getting together and working for full equality with men. Did you know that? Girls like Emily should not send boys out to do things for them. They should go out and do things for themselves.'

'Emily in here?' laughed Daniel. 'I would pay a shilling to see that.'

Muriel squeezed his hand again. 'You know, you talk like boys who are seventeen or eighteen.'

'Is that good?' Daniel asked, hoping that the matter of his real age would not be mentioned.

'Oh yes, you're suave and witty, just like the artists I know.'

Daniel was again at a loss for words. Up until about five minutes ago he had been living the life of a little boy, yet all the while he had apparently looked and sounded like a man. Suddenly Daniel realised that the Germans had entered and sat down near the window. The experience of talking to a girl and even having his hand held had driven away all thoughts of serving king and country, saving parliament and changing the future. He leaned over the table.

'Those people near the window, the five men talking loudly in German,' Daniel whispered. 'Do you know them?'

'Yes. They buy paint at my mother's shop. They're a strange lot.'

'Strange? Why?'

'They buy equal amounts of all colours, including white.'

'Why is that strange?'

'White is used to lighten other colours; artists buy lots more white than anything else. Every week those men over there come along and buy two tubes of everything. They were there today, just when I came home from school. They never buy new brushes, either. Real artists are always spoiling or damaging brushes.'

'Just like people pretending to be artists,' concluded Daniel. 'Somehow it's obvious. Maybe too obvious. Muriel, how do they travel around?'

'They have a big, black coach with shuttered windows.'

Suddenly yet another piece of the puzzle fell into place for Daniel. The artists had eluded Barry by getting into a large coach. No artist travelled in a large coach, hidden from prying eyes by shutters, and Barry had a blind spot for large and expensive coaches unless one was threatening to run him down. Daniel knew that he was a long way from seeing the complete picture, however. If the Germans were pretending to be Germans, they were probably not real Germans. The Germans were also pretending to be artists but were probably not real artists, either. Pretending. The five men were being just a little too blatant about their act, almost as if they were pretending to be pretending. Look at them carefully, and they seem suspicious, thought Daniel. On the other hand, try to recall something about them, and you would remember only that they were Germans pretending to be artists. Something did not add up.

Daniel glanced at Muriel. She was the daughter of a widowed Australian shopkeeper, but pretending to be a young artist from Paris. Why? Because it made her a little exotic, because people took her more seriously than they would if she were merely Australian. German artists. That was like Scottish chefs or French engineers. The idea left people shaking their heads rather than suspicious. Nobody would look too closely until there was a reason, like a major bombing. Nobody would look, unless they had been told to by someone from the future. The Germans all had bushy eyebrows, beards and bulbous noses, and were heavily built, while not actually fat. What was significant about this? It was as if they had all been disguised in the same way. If they were disguised, were they even Germans?

Barry appeared at the door, clutching his bag as if he had very nearly lost it recently.

'Do you know that boy in the doorway?' Daniel asked urgently, fighting down the reflex to pull his hand away from Muriel's.

'Do I ever!' she snorted. 'He came into the shop last month and tried to have my mum stock some dirty postcards as "artistic supplies".'

Daniel suddenly decided that he had to protect Muriel from Barry. After all, she had been charming to him.

'His name is Barry the Bag. He is bad company, but he is a friend of mine.'

'Yes, I saw you with him last time,' said Muriel. 'You … are you in trouble with the police? I mean everyone who knows Barry seems to be in trouble with the police.'

'One might say I'm in trouble,' replied Daniel, half expecting that she would bound up and run before Barry reached the table.

'Oh my, magical!' breathed Muriel, squeezing Daniel's hand again, her eyes shining.

Daniel did not even try to guess what Barry might think when confronted by the sight of an older girl holding hands with him. Barry stopped before the table, blinked, then gave Muriel a suspicious glare and sat down.

'So wot's up, Danny Boy?' he asked.

'Barry, this is Muriel, she's an artist. Muriel, meet Barry, he's ... actually don't ask.'

'We've met,' said Muriel.

'Danny Boy, wot ya doin'?' pleaded Barry, glancing about nervously. 'She only sells paint for her mum, she's no artist.'

'I'm more artistic than your crummy French postcards!' snapped Muriel.

'So, Barry, what happened with the constable?' interjected Daniel.

'Constable?' whispered Muriel, again awe-struck.

'Talked me way out, Dan Man. Barry the Bag 'as stuff for trade, ya know? Not sayin' wot I traded, though, not with 'er listenin'. Wot's the German story?'

'Muriel told me something about them.'

'Yeah? Wot?'

Daniel suddenly noticed that the Germans were getting up to leave.

'Hurry now, they're going!' he hissed to Barry. 'Get the bike, go to the lane where we lost them the other day. Follow a big, black coach when it comes out. They will be in it.'

'Danny Boy, artists can't afford coaches like that.'

'They are not artists, they're probably not even Germans. Now hurry!'

Daniel was actually out of the café before he realised that Muriel was still with him.

'What are you doing here?' he hissed in alarm, pulling her back into a shop's doorway.

'This is so exciting, I want to help.'

'It's dangerous, too! We could get arrested, or even shot!'

'Oh, really, truly?' breathed Muriel, the glazed, dreamy look returning to her eyes.

So, some girls actually like unsavoury, suspicious people, Daniel decided in amazement. Muriel had held his hand twice, and seemed fascinated by him. Now he had a protective arm around her shoulders. It had to be something about him specifically, because she had not shown any interest in Barry, and Barry was a lot more unsavoury and suspicious. Maybe she likes me, Daniel decided. I'd die for a girl who likes me. She would be someone who could really appreciate it.

The coach rumbled past as Daniel and Muriel stood in the shop's doorway. It was very nearly out of sight by the time Barry had returned with the bicycle.

'Where is it?' panted Barry as he pulled up.

'Probably turned off into Fitzroy Street by now!' said Muriel, gazing into the distance with her hands on her hips.

'I'll catch 'em!'

Barry soon vanished into the distance amid the cabs, horses and other bicycles.

'So, um, what happens now?' asked Muriel.

'We do what Sherlock Holmes would have done,' replied Daniel.

Muriel followed Daniel into the laneway where the coach and its driver had been waiting for the Germans to return. Daniel now scandalised her by beginning to lift the lids off the garbage bins.

'Don't, they're filthy!' she cried. 'You'll get typhoid and die like my dad.'

'I'll wash my hands in the horse trough,' said Daniel, making his way from bin to bin. 'Aha, what's this?'

He lifted a neatly wrapped brown paper package from a bin by the string that bound it.

'I ... I wrapped that, this afternoon,' said Muriel. 'The Germans, it was for the Germans. I don't understand. There's a couple of guineas worth of paint in there. Why did they throw it away?'

'So that in a week or so, when the police come to your mother's shop, you will say that they bought paint and spoke like Germans.'

'The police?' gasped Muriel. 'What have the Germans done?'

'Nothing, yet. But they will.'

'What are you going to do now?'

'Find Fox, then walk back to Balaclava Station and take a train home. I have to show this package to some people.'

'Can I help? I'd love to help.'

'What? Muriel! You don't even know that I'm not a criminal.'

'No, but I think you're interesting. Well, nice, too. Too nice to be bad. Well, I mean if you *are* doing something bad, it must be for a good reason.'

She likes me, thought Daniel. She likes me even though I could be a dangerous criminal.

Daniel found and briefed Fox at another café, then left him to his own devices. Muriel offered Daniel a ride to Balaclava Station on her bicycle. Daniel pedalled, while Muriel rode on the seat, holding on to his waist and thus playing havoc with his newly awakened hormones.

For a time they stood on the platform in silence, waiting for the train. Barry reappeared, muttering sullenly that he had lost the coach. He glared at a pocket watch he had stolen from Constable Barrington, then said some very hard words about the efficiency of the railways. Muriel drew Daniel aside.

'Daniel, when will I see you again?' she asked.

'Perhaps tomorrow?'

'Can you tell me anything about who you are, um, shadowing?'

'No! No, it's really very dangerous. I … I can't let you get hurt. That would be too terrible.'

'Oh, Daniel, how sweet of you,' whispered Muriel, slipping her arms around his waist and pressing her head against his. Her breasts also pressed against his chest. Daniel felt his knees turn to jelly. 'I'll keep a lookout for those Germans, or whoever they are,' she continued. 'I can even ask other artists about them.'

'No!'

'Yes! Daniel, I move in artistic circles a lot more than you. Call in at Mother's shop every day, after school, and I shall tell you what I learn.'

'Muriel, look, I'm helping people who are … who are not covered by laws that apply to us. It's complicated. Messy.'

'Who are they, Daniel?'

'Don't ask. Just … just forget this evening.'

'No! This is so exciting, I want to help.'

'You can't.'

'But I will. You know where to find me.'

The train arrived. Muriel pressed her lips against Daniel's. Daniel's mind declared that being kissed by the beautiful Muriel Baker was far too much to cope with without prior warning, and ceased to function. He had the vague impression of being dragged onto the train by Barry, then waving to Muriel as the train pulled away.

'Gotta watch them women,' muttered Barry unhappily, one hand on his bag, the other on the station bicycle.

'I was watching Muriel very carefully,' replied Daniel dreamily.

'Ya meant to be watchin' the bleedin' Germans!'

'I was. I learned that they travel in the black coach, remember?'

'Yeah, well, ya might've learned more if ya weren't kissin' that girl.'

'Her lips were so soft. Some poet once said his girl's lips were like petals falling off a rose. Muriel's lips were just like that.'

'Danny Boy! Get a grip! She's a danger.'

'Because of Muriel, we are going to learn more than ever. She is going to spy for us.'

Barry put his hands to his face, then suddenly remembered that he had let his bag go and snatched for it. The train stopped at Ripponlea, but nobody else got into the carriage.

'Best not to have nothin' to do with women,' muttered Barry.

'Barry, I just can't understand you. You have a bag

full of things for … for, well, you know, doing scandalous things with girls, and yet you're too scared to even say hullo to a real girl!'

'I'm not scared!'

'Yes you are!'

'She's not one of us!'

'Is Emmy one of us?'

'No – Yes! I mean, she's not a real girl. No, no, I mean she don't act like a real girl. Like you'd never think of doin' nothin' with her. I mean of a morally rude nature. That Muriel, though, she's a worry. She'd 'ave ya betrayin' king an' country for a smile, Danny Boy.'

'Muriel held my hand, she kissed me,' said Daniel, gazing out of the window. 'I would die for her.'

'See? See?'

'But I would not betray the Empire for her.'

'Yeah? Hah!'

At Gardenvale two women got into the carriage, and the boys fell silent. The next station was North Brighton. Daniel and Barry got out. Barry's father was collecting the tickets, and was clearly not happy about the situation. Barry was slapped across the ear and shouted at, then left in charge of the station while his father went off to the pub. Daniel waited nearby until they were alone again.

'Look Barry, I think we can manage at Acland Street without you, now that we have Muriel,' began

Daniel, who was genuinely worried about getting Barry into trouble.

'No! No way in the world.'

'But …'

'I said no! Danny Boy, if I was frightened of me old man, d'ya think I'd be any good against the Germans?'

'I saw what happened just now.'

'Yeah, well, sometimes ya just gotta take it quietly. We're just boys. Danny Boy gets caned, Barry the Bag gets a thick ear. People thinks we're in our place and learned our lesson. They leave us alone, and it's then we're free. A beatin' buys us freedom, Dan Man.'

'I suppose you know best.'

'Oh yeah, Barry's got smarts. Speakin' of smarts, take a bit more advice from the Bag, an' don't tell yer sister about Muriel.'

Daniel had no intention of doing anything of the kind. As he walked home from the station, he realised that Barry had been right in his own curious way. Muriel was nothing like Emily. Muriel was the symbol of all women, normal women, not Emily or his mother. Daniel wanted someone to die for. Muriel was worthy of that. BC would have been worthy of it, except that he was a boy, and now that he had been kissed by Muriel, Daniel would only die for BC if the Empire's fate depended on it. Suddenly

Daniel's self-destructive streak asserted itself. BC was the ideal boy, just as Muriel was the ideal girl. One day BC would meet Muriel. Daniel would not have a chance. BC and Muriel were meant for each other. Daniel decided that it was his destiny to bring them together, to sacrifice his happiness for them. It was so tragic that it was wonderful. Muriel had showed Daniel charm, so he would give her BC. Somehow it was a very good exchange, as far as Daniel was concerned.

7

COMMANDER

As the days before the opening of parliament slipped away, Emily became increasingly desperate for BC to get his health back and resume command of the crew. In one sense, her rule was a brilliant success. People followed orders, did things without her parents knowing, collected evidence and made notes. In general, she managed to hold the crew together and make it function efficiently. On the other hand, they learned nothing that might help them to change the future.

Each day BC revived sufficiently to go to the bathroom and eat, then Fox would give him another tablet and he would lapse back into the coma that seemed not far removed from death. It was not until the day before the opening of parliament that Fox ran out of tablets. To Emily's immense relief, BC awakened, collected the nondescript clothes that Fox had bought for him, and went downstairs for a bath.

Locked in her room, Emily contemplated Barry's French postcards. Girls wearing not so much as a scrap of ribbon lay in a variety of poses, all of which suggested vulnerability, along with something else.

This must be what the novelists call allure, thought Emily as she contemplated a girl lying on a bed with her head and arm draped over the edge. Just suppose I get it wrong, what would he think? Suddenly flinging the card down, Emily began to undress. Before long she was draping herself across her bed in a variety of poses suggested by the cards, and feeling very foolish indeed. On the other hand, Emily was nothing if not diligent, and with the aid of the little collection of postcards and a hand mirror, she spent a half-hour battering away at her inhibitions until she could at least lie naked, just as the models had for the photographer. Suddenly a flush of prickly heat burned through her as she made a very important decision.

'I am going to do it with him!' she whispered aloud.

As she began to dress again, the thought crossed her mind that girls might have to do something other than merely drape themselves decoratively over a bed before the eyes of their sweetheart. 'The male becomes aroused,' the book had said. Aroused by what? Emily now wondered. Having finished dressing, she realised that certain items of clothing were a little involved to remove. The stairs creaked with the weight of BC as he returned from the bathroom.

What to do? wondered Emily. Well, horrid, immoral girls like Muriel Baker know what to do, but there's nothing that they can do that I can't.

Another five minutes went into discarding her lace-up boots in favour of shoes with buckles, and replacing her blouse with one whose buttons popped open easily. After a last inspection of herself before the dressing table mirror, she opened the door of her bedroom, then immediately pulled it shut again, turned, and tidied all of Barry's French postcards into her underwear drawer. Suddenly realising that sketches of BC and a BC doll were still in full view, Emily bundled the evidence of her affection for the young officer from the future into the drawers of her dressing table. Yet again she looked around the room, then stared at the door.

'Tomorrow you go into battle, my sweetheart, and you will die,' she told the youth beyond the door. 'You must, *must* go with this memory of me, and of how much I love you.'

Emily stepped out into the corridor, pulled the door closed behind her, then went down the stairs. The groom was away, driving the carriage for her parents. Martha could be heard splashing in the bathroom and singing music hall songs, and Fox and Daniel were away on missions that she had arranged. There is no possibility of interruption, Emily thought as she climbed the stairs again. She reached the upstairs passage just as BC came down the stairs from the garret.

'Miss Emily, good evening, I was about to come in search of you,' said BC, spreading his hands to show off his new clothes. 'What do you think?'

'I, ah, a little dowdy, but very good,' said Emily, her pulse racing and her body burning with something akin to fever.

'Dowdy, yes, that is good. I need to blend in with the crowds. I must confess that I was at my most awkward on parade grounds. I felt very conspicuous in dress uniform.'

'I am sure you would look just stunning in dress uniform,' said Emily truthfully, suddenly aware that the muscles of her left leg were beginning to spasm.

'Are any of the others home?' BC asked.

'No, but please, come into my room. I need to tell you about everything that has been happening.'

BC followed Emily into her bedroom, and as she sat on the bed, he went to the stool before her dressing table.

'No, please, sit here on the bed,' said Emily firmly.

'But —'

'It is the manners, manners, yes, it is good manners — that is, bad manners to give a guest a less comfortable seat.'

BC sat on the bed, close enough for Emily to feel the heat from his body. In a way he is touching me already, she thought. This is romantic, this really is so romantic.

'BC, the crew is in good condition, they are all working well together, and have been spying on the Germans in Acland Street. Fox has been posing as an artist, and he does very beautiful charcoal sketches, you know. Oh, and each night he has been slipping into the Exhibition Buildings and checking the roof.'

'Are there any explosives hidden there as yet?'

'No, there are only wires and decorations. The German artists do not do anything suspicious, except act like German artists. It is all a terrible puzzle to me, and I am at my wits' end trying to make plans. I am longing for you to take over again and ... oh my goodness, I'm sorry, I forgot to ask how your poor tummy ... um, stomach is feeling.'

'It is much improved. I believe that I could even go to the Exhibition Buildings tomorrow.'

'Oh wonderful, wonderful!' exclaimed Emily, putting a hand on BC's arm for a moment. 'I feel so wretched, trying to hold everything together, yet not making any progress.'

'It seems to me that you have done very well,' said BC sincerely. 'Where are the others at this moment?'

'Fox is checking the Exhibition Buildings one last time. Are you sure that the roof was not brought down with cannons hidden in nearby houses?'

'History is very clear that bombs were used. Please go on.'

'Daniel and Barry are in St Kilda, watching the Germans while selling rude postcards to people. Daniel sold one to the vicar yesterday afternoon. He said it was so embarrassing when they recognised each other.'

How, oh how, do people first raise the subject of doing it? Emily screamed to herself. I should have left my hand on his arm, or perhaps at least started patting it. Is patting arousing? Stupid book! It left all the important things out.

'In every battle, there must be casualties,' BC was saying. 'What else?'

'I told everyone to have a special scheme in case nothing else worked. Nobody was to tell anyone else what they planned, in case we got captured and tortured for information. If all else fails, I plan to use the, um, plasma rifle to start fires and frighten people, so that everyone runs away before parliament sits. I mean, they might bomb some later attempt to open parliament, but that is the best that I can do.'

'That is very impressive,' said BC, looking Emily straight in the eyes.

'Truly?'

'Yes, although using the plasma weapon would be a little extreme, and probably cause more problems than it solves. Emily, you have done so well that I am genuinely reluctant to take over from you again.'

'Oh BC, so you *will* take over again!' exclaimed Emily, putting her hands on BC's shoulders. 'Thank you, thank you so much!'

BC put a clenched fist on his chest in salute. 'You were a good choice for my DBC, and I sincerely hope that you will stand with the rest of us tomorrow.'

Now or never, thought Emily, who then slid her arms around BC's back and jammed her lips against his. The youth gave a spasm of alarm, but Emily held him all the more tightly. My intentions must definitely be plain by now, she thought. She pulled her head back abruptly.

'We have two hours before anyone comes home, and Martha always takes ages in the bath!' said Emily urgently, looming over the thoroughly alarmed BC, who was by now on his back on her bed.

'No, no, this is unseemly,' he insisted. 'And besides –'

'Not another word!' said Emily, gathering up her skirts up and exposing her legs to male eyes for the first time in her life as she straddled BC. 'Tomorrow you go into battle, and I want you to have this from me before you die. This is what happens with girls and heroes. I've read novels about it.'

BC looked for all the world as if he were about to call out for help. Emily decided to take matters into her own hands, seeing that her sweetheart was being too much of a gentleman about taking the initiative. Putting a hand on his stomach to feel where the bandages were, she began to work her way upwards, popping the buttons of his shirt open as she went. Surely this is arousing him, Emily thought with desperation. Her fingers caressed smooth, soft skin that overlaid iron-hard muscles, then ...

It seemed like hours had passed, but in fact the interval had only been a dozen or so seconds. Feeling wretched and utterly humiliated, Emily sat cowering in a corner of the bedroom with her hands over her eyes, shutting out the nightmare before her.

'And besides, I am a girl,' mumbled BC, sounding very apologetic.

Emily gradually spread her fingers and looked up. BC was buttoning up her shirt.

'I do apologise for the deception, but it is just too hard for a girl to move freely in this time and place, especially in your society.'

'There are a lot of dangerous thugs about,' responded Emily.

'I know. I've killed two,' replied BC.

With that BC got up, walked over to Emily, and held out her hand.

'Come, sit. The bed is more comfortable.'

'I hope you realise that I was trying to give my maidenhead to you just now,' said Emily in a tight, terse voice as BC led her across the room.

'I really am flattered, if that is any comfort to you.'

'It is not, but thank you anyway. I … I cannot believe that a girl could be the commander over so many boys.'

'A century from now, girls will be free of the restraints that they presently experience.'

'It sounds like paradise,' said Emily wistfully. 'I feel so trapped.'

'Trapped?' laughed BC. 'All of us are trapped.'

'Twaddle. You are not trapped, you are gloriously free.'

'Not so. In the future I was trapped in a mad military empire that would have sent me to my death, with my eight crew, before I turned sixteen. In your time I am trapped in the clothes of a boy, because I would seem like a freak as a girl warrior. Fox is trapped by his conditioning. He plays the stupid soldier even though he is more intelligent than any of us. Barry is trapped within his own mind by poverty and those who despise him, yet he is so astoundingly resourceful that I am not sure how to make use of him.'

'Barry?' gasped Emily.

'Yes. Then there is Daniel. Daniel is so trapped by you and your mother that he thinks the only way to win a girl's approval is to die for her.'

'No!'

'Yes. It is very unhealthy. Out of all of you, I worry about him the most.'

BC had raised a gaggle of intensely personal issues that Emily usually avoided as carefully as her mother and father avoided the subject of sex. She decided upon a change of subject.

'Well, Liore, the army of the future must be very good at training people if you and Fox are any guide. You fight so well, even when injured and outnumbered.'

'It all evolved from rowing crews,' explained BC. 'Eight cadets would row the shell, the boat, and someone small and light would be the cox and steer. It did not matter if the cox was male or female, as long as they were light, and could command with absolute certainty and inspire total commitment. Rowing develops that sort of absolute team loyalty and coordination between members of a crew. People in the Empire's military academies realised that it was the best way to develop teams of warriors who worked together perfectly. One began by commanding a boat crew, which then became a battle squad.'

'And if the Battle Commander rebels, the crew always follows?' asked Emily.

'No other BC has ever rebelled,' replied BC, looking and sounding oddly crushed.

'Oh.'

'I led the rebellion, my crew followed. I was so

proud of them; it was all that allowed me to bear the disgrace. We had won the antipodean boat race championships, and were hailed by King Charles himself as the fittest, strongest and most disciplined war academy crew in the Australian Commonwealth, and a model for all other cadets to follow. In just ninety seconds all that had changed. We knew the winning crew was to be honoured by being made part of the guard for the Flinders Chronologic Research Station for an afternoon, and we made a desperate plan to get back to this time, before the storm that was the Twentieth Century.'

'Station?' said Emily, trying very hard to understand. 'So there was a time train there?'

'A time weapon, not a train. We rebelled during the parade in our honour, shot our way into the laboratory, set bombs to destroy the time weapon, then … then the two of us who were still alive vanished into time before the bombs went off.'

'You used a time weapon without having lessons first?'

'Weapons are easy to use. Repairing the damage they do is the hard part, and we did a lot of damage. I betrayed my academy, my family, my class, my king and my empire. My name will be cursed forever. I am command class, and I have betrayed command class. I led my crew against no enemy; instead we destroyed the most important weapon in the British Empire.'

'Well, I still think you are brave and noble!' declared Emily.

'Why?' asked BC with a shrug. 'I am a traitor, Emily. Fox and I are both traitors.'

Emily had to stop to think about just why she still admired the dangerous killer who was sitting on her bed and wallowing in self-pity. At school one had to be part of a group, or one was a social outcast. The girls in Emily's group wore three ruffles at the necks of their blouses and read Jane Austin. Emily did not like ruffles and preferred Jules Verne as an author, yet she went on pretending otherwise, rather than leaping into the abyss and losing her friends. BC had been far braver. She had leaped, she had broken out of her trap. Emily wondered whether she could do the same, or even do something to help Daniel.

'Fighting your own people is a much braver thing than fighting an enemy,' Emily said slowly. 'Nobody is there to cheer you on, and nobody will weep when you fall.'

'What is weep?' asked BC.

Something gave way within Emily, and she felt herself beginning to crumble from within. At her first sobs BC sat up immediately, wide-eyed and thoroughly alarmed. She can cope with everything except sadness, observed Emily.

'Weep ... is when you are very sad,' Emily sniffled. 'I'm very sad now. Very sad ... because seven strong, noble, brave, handsome, well-mannered boys, the boys from your crew ... are *dead*.'

BC squirmed.

'Four of them were girls,' she announced softly, hunching over and staring at her tightly clasped hands.

Now Emily's tears came out in a very impressive flood.

'What does one do about weep syndrome?' asked BC, sounding concerned yet helpless, and making no attempt to touch Emily. 'Is it like battle fatigue or post-combat stress?'

'BC, just shut up, will you?' shouted Emily. 'Just ... no, no, I'm sorry. You don't understand, you can't understand. Just leave me alone, this will pass.'

'My people died bravely. They took sixty guards with them into the House of Death,' said BC, trying to comfort her in the only way that she knew. 'Actually it might have been sixty-one. I am sure JetS5 hit two with one shot before she died.'

The scene from the projector machine flashed through Emily's mind. She fought down the urge to be sick, and wondered how she could ever have thought that war was a glorious adventure.

'Is that meant to make me feel better?' she asked, her voice becoming steady again.

'Did I say something ill-mannered?' asked BC in turn.

'No, no, you could never say anything ill-mannered. This is for me to understand. Please, help me to understand. Tell me about how you rebelled.'

'There is little to tell. FoxS3 did forbidden studies when he was allowed into libraries to read of technical matters. He learned real history, dissident opinions, even songs sung in old courtly, the form that we are speaking now. He learned a song about rowing. It was from a time when rowing was a sport, not a way to bond the most deadly of our warrior squads. It was such a sweet little song, all about sunny days on the river, doing things together, and ties that bind friends forever. He was singing it one day when the provosts heard him. They put him on a charge, and he was flogged.'

'Oh, no!'

'The actual charge was speaking in courtly – that is forbidden to his class. The rest of the crew watched. He was cut down from the triangle; then, with the blood streaming from his back, he had to apologise to us for bringing disgrace upon the crew. For me, that was the end. I started to think about things. I started to get ideas.'

'Dangerous people, girls with ideas. Father keeps telling me to avoid them.'

'For me, nothing was ever the same again. We of the crew all knew each other, totally and completely. I knew that the crew believed in me, so if I thought something was worth fighting for, they would fight alongside me, and even die. I thought about FoxS3 being flogged, and then I thought about the academy, the Empire, the war, and even about saving the world. Out on the water, rowing, in the privacy of the boat, I had discussions with my crew. I told them that it was the provosts who ought to have been flogged, not FoxS3. FoxS3 said that destroying the world to save it from the Germans was immoral. StrokeS8 said that he would be willing to die as a traitor, in disgrace, to save the world. The rest agreed. Now seven of us are indeed dead. Only Fox and I are left, trying to change our yesterday.'

Emily took a very deep breath. 'No, not just Fox and you,' she declared. 'Daniel, myself and Barry make up a coxed four with the two of you. I know I am not much of a warrior, BC, but nobody will be more loyal or try to work more perfectly with the rest of your crew. Since I discovered that you are a girl too, I have realised that I need no boys to free me from my cage or solve my problems for me. You are the perfect boy, yet you are a girl. This may be the most important thing I ever learn.'

'But I am not perfect.'

'Yes you are,' said Emily as she reached out to BC. 'Now come here.'

'I am a girl too, remember?' gasped BC in alarm.

'Girls are allowed to do this,' she explained, putting her arms around BC. 'It is called a hug, it makes sad people feel better.'

'It is therapy for weeping syndrome?' asked BC.

'Yes, but close friends just do it anyway.'

The day of parliament's opening began as something of a blur for Emily. After the events of the previous night, she had managed to get no sleep at all, and was intent on surviving the day, rather than directing it. One thought was, however, foremost in her mind. BC was a girl. A century in the future, girls were allowed to be stylish, dashing, brave, and even heroic. Girls could lead. That sounded as unlikely as Barry the Bag being a battle commander, yet BC was the proof.

During the night Emily had managed to deduce that she was so attracted to BC because she wanted to *be* like her, not because she desired her. Perhaps many girls courted dashing and heroic boys because they wished to be near the sort of person they secretly wished they could become. Obviously boys of the future would follow a girl into battle. What about boys of 1901? It was only now that Emily suddenly realised how she might extract considerably more dedication and loyalty from Daniel and Barry.

While Mr and Mrs Lang were still asleep, Emily ejected her brother from his bed and told him to get dressed. She then marched him down to the railway station. As usual, Barry was at the ticket window.

'Thought the gentry was goin' to parlyment by carriage?' began Barry cheerily, as Daniel and Emily stood before him.

'Come out onto the platform, Barry, we need to have a serious talk,' snapped Emily.

'Cor, wot's I done now?'

'Nothing. This is about what you *will* be doing.'

Out on the platform, and away from inquisitive ears, Emily stood before the two boys with her hands on her hips.

'Now then, this is the day that the future can be saved,' she began. 'All of us must do everything we can to help our battle commander, Miss Liore BC, to –'

'That thing's a *girl?*' exclaimed Barry.

'I will thank you not to refer to your battle commander and my best friend as a thing.'

'We *are* still talking about BC, are we not?' asked Daniel, whose face had suddenly lost all trace of colour, and whose voice was barely audible.

'BC is sick and wounded, but she still has to fight the bombers. It is up to us to help her however we can.'

'Bleedin' 'ell. I'd never live it down if some daft baggage got shot instead of me!' declared Barry. 'I mean blokes are supposed to get shot first, Danny Boy told me.'

'Are you sure she's a girl?' asked Daniel.

'You have my word for it,' replied Emily. 'Barry, where will you be today?'

'Helpin' Foxy, an' workin' on me secret plan, like ya said. I've got Lurker the Worker to –'

'Don't tell me! A secret plan is meant to be secret.'

'Can't I come along and fight?' pleaded Barry. 'I feel like such a pansy, lettin' some girl get shot at instead of me, like even though she's stronger than I am, an' killed more coves than I've eaten hot pies, and –'

'What about me?' pleaded Daniel. 'I could stand in front of her or something if people started shooting.'

'Hang on, why can't I do nothin' brave?' demanded Barry.

'Well, you can stand in front of Emmy,' said Daniel.

'Wot? Waste me life on … no offence Miss …'

I have them, thought Emily. To save the world, the boys are willing to fight. To save BC, they are willing to die. To save BC, I suppose I am, too.

BC accompanied the Lang family in their carriage as they made the journey to the Exhibition Buildings. She had removed some parts from her gun so that it was shorter, and looked more like a pistol. Concealed under her coat, nobody would have guessed that it was there. Fox had not come home at all, but via his telegraph device he had reported to BC that he was watching for the Germans somewhere in Carlton, and that no explosives had been planted in the Exhibition Buildings during the night. Emily actually dozed in the carriage, leaning against BC. By now the idea of physical contact with the warrior from the future no longer had the same allure. She was shaken awake as they were getting out of the carriage. Then the groom drove it away, leaving them to mingle with the crowds.

'Now then, everyone, I have a special treat arranged,' Mr Lang announced as they strolled together into the Exhibition Gardens. 'Lieutenant, that even includes you.'

'But Sir, I am to participate in the ceremony,' replied BC at once.

'Are you indeed? Well, I do wish I had known that in advance.'

'I must be going now, but I shall meet with you again when the opening is over.'

With that, BC vanished into the crowd.

'Such a pity about that,' said Mr Lang. 'I have passes for all five of us to get into the actual ceremony.'

Emily's blood went cold, and she was instantly wide awake. By the expression on his face, she could tell that Daniel realised the danger as well.

'There, there, dear, if Liore is part of the ceremony, he will be inside as well,' said Mrs Lang. 'Oh look, there are the Wilsons.'

As the adult Langs stood exchanging pleasantries with their friends, Emily drew Daniel away for a hurried meeting.

'Now what?' demanded Daniel. 'Do we all go in-side and get ourselves killed?'

'Fox found no explosives last night, and the Germans have not been near this place since then,' said Emily. 'Perhaps history has already been changed.'

'I just have a bad feeling about this,' insisted Daniel. 'There are too many people telling me that everything is all right, and you are one of them.'

'I am only telling you what I know.'

'Well, even that much makes me worried.'

'I think we should just do nothing for now.'

'No! That way we are going to be in there when the bombs are meant to bring the roof down.'

Other children were milling about, mostly of parents who had invitations to be inside for the actual opening of the first Australian Parliament. Daniel and Emily were not inclined to talk with them, but they did exchange greetings.

'We should mix with the crowd,' Emily whispered to her brother. 'You never know, perhaps BC will need us.'

'We need to ask BC what to do,' suggested Daniel. 'Come on, let's find her.'

Daniel told their parents that he was bored and wanted to look for his friends.

'Very well, but Emily must go with you, to remind you when to come back,' said Mr Lang. 'If you are late, your mother and I shall go in without you.'

They slipped into the crowd, trying not to look as if they were hurrying. After some minutes of searching they had not found BC, but they did encounter a lot more friends from their schools.

'Oi, Dan Man, how go your prospects?' called a gangly youth wearing a straw boater hat.

Emily knew the speaker to be one of Daniel's classmates, but not one that he was especially friendly with.

'Good prospects for being bored, William,' replied Daniel.

'Ah, so you don't have a pass to get inside?'

'That's just the trouble, I do have a pass. I'll be there for everything.'

'Then you will not be bored.'

'I shall indeed. Hours of speeches, and people clapping only because they are relieved when the speakers finish.'

'What about when the snow starts to fall?'

'It's May, and it's Melbourne,' laughed Daniel. '*You* have a better chance of passing algebra than Melbourne has of getting snow.'

'Oh, but there will be snow, that's why I have my hat.'

'You have your hat because you're daft, William. It's too hot for snow.'

'But what about paper snow?'

'You're still being daft. Snow is made out of ice crystals.'

'Well, I think that a couple of dozen bags on the ceiling full of shredded paper will produce what looks like snow.'

'How did you find out about this?' asked Emily suddenly.

'Dad's company is staging it. Firecrackers will burst dozens of bags of paper scrap on the ceiling, causing a snowstorm inside. Dad's workmen carried them up this morning. Nobody is meant to know, 'cause it's meant to be a special surprise.'

Emily took Daniel by the arm and dragged him out of earshot from the others.

'They must be the bombs!' she hissed.

'But look, people are starting to go in,' replied Daniel.

'I was right, the future cannot be changed!' whispered Emily in desperate frustration.

'Daniel, Daniel!' shouted a female voice.

Emily knew the voice. Judging from Daniel's reaction, he knew it too. Muriel Baker came rushing along the gravel path toward them, her hair brushed out and a blue beret on her head.

'Daniel, the Germans are here!' Muriel announced, taking Daniel's hands in hers. 'Last night I followed them – oh, hullo Emily – last night I followed them on my bicycle. Their beards and noses are false. I saw them peeling their disguises off in an alleyway, and –'

'Daniel Lang, where and when did you meet this, this floozy?' demanded Emily.

'She's not a floozy!' snapped Daniel.

'We've been holding hands for a week,' added Muriel.

'You're courting her?' Emily shrieked at Daniel.

'I didn't see you doing any spying, Emily Lang!' retorted Muriel.

'Daniel! How much did you tell her?' demanded Emily, so outraged that their mission to save the future was forgotten.

'Sorry. I have to put my own plan of last resort into action,' cried Daniel, suddenly breaking away from them.

Muriel tried to run after Daniel, but Emily seized her by the arm. Daniel ran for three policemen who were standing beside a small service door in the side of the building.

'Muriel Baker, how dare you defile my brother's good name?' demanded Emily.

'Let me go!' cried Muriel, slapping Emily across the face. 'Those three policemen are the *Germans*!'

Emily gasped and whirled around, but it was too late.

'Constables, you must get the people out of there!' Daniel shouted as he ran. 'The decorations that were put in the roof this morning, they're bombs; they're going to kill everyone!'

To Emily's astonishment, then horror, she saw the police surround Daniel, clamping a hand over his mouth and pinning his arms behind his back. All three of them looked furtive and fearful as they bundled Daniel through the small door beside them.

'Nothing to worry about, ladies and gentlemen!' called one of the police as he pulled the door shut behind them. 'Just a schoolboy prank.'

For some moments Emily and Muriel stood with their mouths open. Here was proof that the conspiracy was real; here was proof that bombs were in place. Here was also proof that at least the police, and possibly a lot more people, were involved. The idea that the police could not be trusted was all but unthinkable to Emily. She had been brought up to believe that you could always trust a policeman, so what could she do now?

'Silly cow, I tried to warn you but you wouldn't listen!' shouted Muriel.

'Daniel, they just took him away!' gasped Emily. 'Those police.'

'They're not police!'

'But they had uniforms.'

'Give me your measurements and some cloth, and I could turn *you* into a policeman!' shouted Muriel, stamping her foot.

'We have to call the ... the ...' Emily's voice trailed away hopelessly.

'Police?' asked Muriel, who then twisted out of Emily's grip.

'Whatever can we do?' cried Emily.

'Daniel said you are some sort of leader,' said Muriel, pointing in the direction of the door. 'Well he's a prisoner now. What are you going to do? Don't just stand there, lead!'

Just then the three police re-emerged from the door. Emily suddenly pulled herself together.

'Muriel, wait here, watch the policemen, but don't draw attention to yourself. I'll get help.'

Without another word Emily dashed away into the crowd. The stream of people entering the Exhibition Buildings had slowed to a trickle, and her parents were nowhere to be seen. Now Emily could not enter, even if she wanted to. After what had happened to Daniel, she knew there was no point in trying to raise the alarm about the bombs. Deciding that her only chance was to find BC, Emily began a desperate circumnavigation of the Exhibition Buildings, dodging bands, vendors and even a maypole. She saw plenty of her friends from school – then caught sight of BC.

'Liore!' shrieked Emily, and BC turned and strode towards her at once.

'There are new decorations high on the walls, near the ceiling,' began BC as they met.

'I know. Daniel and I learned of them too, but when he tried to tell some policemen, they seized him and locked him away. They called to the crowd that it was a schoolboy prank, and, and he's been holding hands with *Muriel Baker*!'

'Muriel Baker?' asked BC. 'Is she a conspirator?'

'No, she's my classmate, and she's a year older than Daniel, and she's an *artist*!'

'Please, no more, let me think,' said BC, her eyes now wide. 'The police, of course. The conspirators are not Germans!'

'I ... what? But ...'

'Later. Show me the door. Oh, and do you have the pistol?'

'Yes, but —'

'Keep it out of sight, but if you need to use it, flick the safety catch up, and squeeze the trigger, not the trigger guard. Remember to aim it. That's very important.'

They had to hurry right around to the other side of the Exhibition Buildings to reach the door. When they arrived, the three policemen were still there. Emily took BC to Muriel.

'Liore, this is Muriel, and she's, she's a *friend* of Daniel's. Muriel, this is *Miss* Liore.'

Muriel stared at BC, opened her mouth, and managed to say 'Miss?' before words failed her.

'What have the policemen done since I left?' asked Emily.

'Nothing, they've just been standing near the door,' answered Muriel, finally wrenching her gaze away from BC.

'Wait here,' said BC, who then walked straight for the policemen.

'BC, no, they will take you prisoner too!' pleaded Emily, starting after her.

'He's really a girl?' asked Muriel, following them with her head on one side. 'He'd be a stunning boy.'

'Miss Liore certainly knows how to stun people,' said Emily grimly.

'Gentlemen, I believe that you are trying to keep the bombs in the roof a secret,' declared BC cheerily to the police.

There was a brief, confused flurry as the police tried to restrain BC. Emily saw her right elbow strike a jaw, smash back into a nose, then her fist slam into a stomach. BC lifted her third victim onto her shoulder.

'Schoolboy prank,' Emily called cheerily to the astounded onlookers as she searched the coat pockets of the two other policemen, removing their papers.

'Are you absolutely positive he's a girl?' asked Muriel as she and Emily hurried through the door behind BC. 'I mean, I don't know any girls who could do that.'

'Do you know any boys who could do that?' asked Emily.

They found themselves in a kind of servants' entrance. Having jammed the door's lock from inside, BC gave her entire attention to the policeman in her custody. First she removed his gun. He was making a titanic effort to draw breath after her punch to his stomach. BC twisted his arm behind his back, placed her knee against his spine, then twisted his wrist and gently pressed a point near his elbow. The man's mouth dropped open in a grimace of pain so intense that he could not even bring himself to scream.

'My old karate teacher told me that girls do not like to damage people when they fight, yet they are quite happy to inflict extreme pain,' BC explained calmly to the man. 'Actually, I was his best student, and I am truly overjoyed to inflict the most intense and extreme pain imaginable upon traitors to the British Empire.'

BC pressed another point on the man's arm. He began to shudder uncontrollably.

'Actually, if one inflicts pain like this for long enough, the victim dies. As you may have noticed, the victim can no longer breathe because of the shock.'

BC now eased the pressure a little, and the man actually managed to close his mouth.

'Firstly, you are going to tell us where the boy that you seized some minutes ago has been hidden.'

The policeman attempted to struggle. This was a very serious mistake. BC twisted his arm a little further, and pressed a finger against his wrist. A patch of steaming water began to spread out from the area of his trousers. BC eased the pressure a little.

'Second door, right,' the man wheezed. 'Behind … stack … of cases.'

BC released the man, then took from her coat a thing that Emily recognised as part of her death beam weapon.

'This is the converter of my plasma rifle. Without the rest it cannot be fired at maximum power.' She stared meaningfully at her prisoner. 'But it can still stop anything smaller than an elephant.'

She fired down into the flagstone floor. There was a brief squeak-like sound, followed by a sharp blast. A hole big enough to hold a large orange appeared in the bluestone. The policeman stared at it, all but paralysed with terror.

'Now, if I have to fire this thing at you, it will be at your stomach,' said BC with exaggerated gravity. 'You will take a long time to die, and it will be in extreme agony. Will you do as I say?'

Muriel fainted, but Emily caught her and eased her to the floor. The man nodded.

'Then move! Second door, right.'

Daniel was where the man had said, bound and gagged but otherwise unharmed. BC ordered the man to untie him.

8

THIEF

As soon as Daniel caught sight of the haggard, terrified look on the policeman's face, he knew that BC would not be far behind. BC appeared, and ordered Daniel to be untied.

'The decorations ...' Daniel began as the gag came off his mouth.

'We know, Daniel, good work,' said BC.

'That policeman,' began Daniel again.

'He is not a policeman, he just wears the uniform,' said BC. 'Now then, I would advise you and Muriel to look the other way and cover your ears.'

BC seized the policeman and slammed him to the ground again.

'Daniel, you are still looking,' called BC. 'Some people just don't care about losing their breakfast, do they, *Constable*? Now then, I know that you are part of an imperialist supremacist group, dedicated to keeping Australia as a collection of colonies in an empire run directly and centrally by Britain. Yes, I worked all that out for myself. The weakness about rewritten history is that it all looks so neat, tidy, and one-sided. German agents? Not likely. You idiots wanted a war to unite the British Empire, but you will get a war that loses Britain! What is your organisation's name?'

'The ... Sons of Britannia.'

There was a soft snap from the man's arm, followed by a wheeze of pain. Daniel's stomach lurched.

'Now that was very, very silly of you. I already know the answer, you see? There is a nice man out in the bushes of the garden who has already helped me with some of my enquiries. Actually he is a rather nasty man, but no matter. I broke both of his elbows and one of his knees before he decided that ...'

'Lionhearts, the League of British Lionhearts,' wheezed the man.

'See how easy it is? Now then, some more questions, and bear in mind that I already know some of the answers.'

'Anything, only ...'

'Stop, yes, I may stop soon. I find the idea of touching you offensive in the extreme, but one has to endure many hardships in the cause of patriotism. How are the bombs in the roof to be set off?'

'Fuses ... will be lit.'

'Come now, you can do better than that. Short fuses would not give your men time to escape, and long fuses would generate so much smoke that they would be noticed.'

'It's true! Those lighting hands ... not our men ... just hired help. They think it's just fireworks, they don't know. Half-minute fuses.'

With truly astounding speed, BC bound the man's hands behind his back, pulled him to his feet, looped a length of cord around a pipe that ran down the wall, and tied him to the pipe.

'Last question,' asked BC. 'When are those bombs due to be set off?'

'Another quarter-hour.'

BC gagged him.

'DanS2, Emily-DBC, to me!' she said as she made for the door. 'We can still save the day.'

BC had her hand on the door's latch as it burst open, knocking her down and sending her weapon from the future clattering away across the floor. The intruder charged through the door. BC lashed a leg out and tripped him, and he fired blindly but only managed to hit his fellow conspirator, who was tied to the pipe. There was a loud snap as the gunman's head hit the wall. Daniel caught sight of a third man, who was aiming a gun at BC.

'Emmy, fire!' shouted Daniel as he flung himself over the fallen BC.

Two gunshots sounded almost simultaneously, a sharp pop, and a much louder blast. Something tugged at Daniel's upper arm, and he felt a sting. There was the sound of something hitting the floor.

'DanS2, status?' demanded BC, rolling Daniel off.

'My arm,' began Daniel.

'Graze, non-lethal, grab hold, apply pressure. Emily-DBC, eyes, shut! DanS2, escort her outside.'

Daniel discovered Muriel in the corridor, sitting on the floor and shaking her head to clear it. He propped Emily against the wall and tried to lift Muriel, while still clutching his bleeding arm.

'Fainted, I fainted,' said Muriel. 'What happened?'

'I shot someone,' Emily whispered.

'I got shot,' said Daniel.

'You shot my Daniel, you stupid cow?' cried Muriel.

'I killed a man,' said Emily, ignoring her.

'Not me,' mumbled Daniel.

'You need a bandage,' said Muriel as she began to rip a strip of cloth from her petticoat.

The thought of being bandaged by a strip of Muriel's petticoat was somehow so erotic that it made Daniel's head spin. Dropping to his knees, he eased his coat off. There was a deep, ominous humming from within the stores room.

'Am I allowed to know what is going on yet?' asked Muriel as she began to bandage Daniel's arm.

'Some really bad people have put bombs in the roof, and they plan to blow up the Exhibition Buildings when parliament's opening,' said Daniel. 'We're trying to stop them.'

The issues raised by those two sentences were far more than Muriel could assimilate at short notice, so she seemed to grasp for a sensible conclusion instead.

'I ... but we are inside the Exhibition Buildings, and parliament is about to open.'

'Yes.'

'And you have not stopped them yet?'

'Not yet, no ...'

'Should we not get outside?'

Just then BC came out of the room, holding her plasma weapon. She pulled the door shut behind her.

'What happened?' asked Daniel.

'One was shot by the fool who smashed in the door, and the one who did the shooting stumbled into the wall and broke his neck. The third ...'

'Would it help if I said it was an accident?' asked Emily guiltily.

'Miss Emily, next time you want to distract some-one with a gunshot, fire into the ceiling.'

'I thought policemen might have armoured coats, like your uniform.'

'Only in a hundred years from now.'

Muriel tied off Daniel's bandage.

'Will the third chap be all right?' asked Daniel.

'Not without a heart. I put my weapon on thermal disruption and turned it on the bodies. There is only ash and steam in there now.'

BC then bent something in the latch of the outer door and locked it again.

'You, Muriel Baker,' said BC, taking out one of the dead men's guns. 'If you stand with Daniel, then you are under my command. Take this pistol. If anyone forces that outer door, shoot them.'

'Shoot them?' asked Muriel, shrinking away from her against Daniel. 'I could never kill anyone.'

'Then aim for the stomach,' advised BC.

'That means they stay alive,' said Daniel.

'Sometimes,' said BC. 'Stand here, guard the door.'

'You mean I have to stay inside?' asked Muriel, taking the gun from BC by the barrel.

'Hold it by the handle,' said Daniel, reversing the gun for her.

'The trigger's the thing inside the loop,' added Emily.

'Quickly, up those steps, they lead to an access platform,' said BC.

'Daniel, I'm only staying inside because I love you!' Muriel called after them.

'I killed a man,' whispered Emily as they ran, her eyes still wide with shock.

'You may have to do it again,' said BC, handing the plasma gun to her. 'Look after this.'

'She loves me!' panted Daniel, as much to annoy Emily as to affirm his first romance.

The access platform was already occupied by five nattily dressed men, who were innocent bystanders in the wrong place at the wrong time. BC's foot swept the feet out from under the first man so fast that he fell and struck the back of his head. He was still falling when the tip of her boot struck the second man in the jaw, instantly dropping him into unconsciousness. At this stage she seemed to leap into the air, spin in a flat circle, and land the heel of her boot against the third man's temple. By now the fourth man had made the mind-numbingly stupid mistake of trying to seize BC. She promptly smashed her forehead down on the bridge of his nose. The fifth man tried to flee.

'I would not try to leave,' warned Emily, pointing both of her guns at the man.

'That shiny one really, really hurts,' added Daniel.

As the man hesitated, BC stepped up behind him, spun him about, and struck his chin with her elbow. With efficient, disciplined fingers, BC attached a small telescope to her gun, then scanned the upper walls.

'Those bomb packets are all over the place,' she exclaimed softly. 'And smoke. There is smoke!'

'The fuses are already lit!' hissed Daniel.

'It's too late!' exclaimed BC. 'Back, hurry!'

'My parents!' exclaimed Daniel.

'Nothing can save them. Run!'

They dashed back down the stairs, and bolted

along the corridor to where Muriel was still waiting.

'... twenty-five, twenty-six, won't make it,' cried BC, 'twenty-eight, twenty-nine ... Down. Lie flat!'

The four of them flung themselves on the flag-stones. They waited, flat on the floor. Daniel grasped for Muriel's hand.

'Thirty-five, thirty-six,' counted BC.

'Muriel, I love you too,' said Daniel.

'For goodness sake,' muttered Emily between clenched teeth.

'Forty-one, forty-two,' said BC, then she stopped counting and looked up.

'Did he not say half-minute fuses?' asked Daniel.

'He did indeed,' said BC, getting to her feet and striding back up the corridor. The others followed, including Muriel.

Daniel saw that BC had her coat unbuttoned, and was holding her hand over a spreading red patch at her stomach. Back at the platform, they found that one of the five men had just returned to his senses. BC trained her gun between his eyes.

'It would be an awfully good idea to stay quiet and lie still,' said Emily, hurrying up with her own pistol.

BC struck the man unconscious again, then scanned the packages high on the walls with her telescopic sights.

'The fuses have burned down and gone out,' she observed. 'The bombs have not gone off.'

For some moments they stood in silence.

Somewhere in the distance, they could hear the Duke of Cornwall and York declaring the parliament to be open.

'Oh, Daniel, how romantic,' squealed Muriel. 'Thank you for getting me in here to actually see it happen.'

'They never reached this part of the ceremony!' said BC above the noise of the cheering that followed. 'History *has* changed. We should leave, quickly and quietly.'

Before they went outside again, Muriel ripped more of her petticoat off and bound the cloth over BC's bandages. BC re-buttoned her coat. Out in the grounds again, they watched the dignitaries and guests that had come so near to death streaming out to continue the day's celebrations. Bands were playing and people were still cheering.

'Over there, those four worried-looking men near the door,' said BC. 'Do you think they are wondering where their friends dressed as policemen have gone?'

'I'd rather not ask,' said Daniel. 'Two of them look a bit like the Germans, with their disguises off.'

'Try to remember their faces,' said BC.

'I killed a man,' said Emily.

'Emily!' hissed BC softly. 'Take hold of your nerve. All warriors feel guilt after a battle. It is only natural. You are still breathing, but those who stood against you are dead. You wonder why you survived and they did not, and you feel guilty about it. I feel it too, but put it out of your mind for now. And you, Daniel, you have faced death three times in the past quarter-hour, and now shock and terror are catching up with you. I can see it in your eyes, and in the way your hands are starting to shake. We need to leave here so that I can counsel you.'

'Counsel us?' he asked.

'Talk you out of the shock that both of you have entered. I suggest that we walk to the railway station; we can talk in private that way. Emily, find your parents, tell them Daniel caught his arm on a projecting nail, tearing his coat and cutting himself.'

'I'll go with her. I'll say I saw it all,' declared Muriel, as she helped Daniel back into his coat.

'Very good,' said BC. 'Daniel, stay with me.'

'Mother and Father will be furious because we did not go in with them,' said Daniel, staring after Muriel and Emily as they hurried off into the crowd.

'I imagine the bombs would have annoyed them a lot more,' replied BC.

'You are bleeding again,' said Daniel. 'What shall we do?'

'Some stitches tore a little with all the action, and blood seeped through the tears,' she said, unbuttoning her coat to check the bleeding. 'It is no worse than a nosebleed, and Muriel's extra bandaging will hold for now.'

'No worse than a nosebleed?' exclaimed Daniel.

'Keep your voice down, we cannot afford to draw attention to ourselves.'

'Oi, Muriel's waving. I do believe she has seen Mother and Father.'

With that, BC buttoned her jacket and led the way forward. Daniel noted at once that his parents looked rather grim.

'Ah, Mr and Mrs Lang, I do apologise!' BC declared as they approached the Langs. 'I thought that Emily, Daniel, and Muriel would like to see the ceremony from a special viewing platform, but you had gone inside before I could get word to you.'

'Oh, a special platform?' asked Mr Lang, brightening at once.

'It was very romantic,' added Emily, who managed a strained smile.

'But I was their chaperone,' added Daniel, still glancing about for British German artists disguised as policemen.

'So was I,' added Muriel with a very broad smile.

'Oh, then that is quite all right,' said Mr Lang. 'Did you hear the Duke declare the parliament open?'

'Indeed we did, Sir,' replied BC.

'Wonderful, just wonderful,' added Mrs Lang. 'So historic, so grand, so romantic.'

'I thought that we four might walk back to

Flinders Street Station through the city centre,' said BC. 'I would like to look at all the decorations that have been put up to celebrate the opening of parliament.'

They were soon alone again, walking along Exhibition Street. BC explained about a medical condition that would not be identified and named for some decades to come.

'It will be called post-traumatic stress syndrome in about seventy years. Daniel, you made a decision to die, you threw yourself across me, fully expecting to be shot and be killed. Now you cannot quite accept that you are still alive.'

'I … I suppose so,' conceded Daniel. 'I know it sounds silly.'

'It is not silly. You were willing to die to save me, and for that I thank you. Emily, the angel of death was so close that he brushed Daniel and me with his wings. Your shot sent him on his way, with the soul of another.'

'But I killed the man. It was truly horrid.'

'If you had enjoyed it, I would have cut you down where you stood. I do not tolerate murderers in my crew.'

That thought sobered Daniel considerably, yet somehow heartened him as well. Muriel stared at BC as they walked, frowning with confusion.

'You don't really like fighting and killing, do you?' Muriel asked.

'Fighting and killing are like wiping one's bottom. You have to do it from time to time, so you must learn how to do it properly or things could become very unpleasant. On the other hand, there are more important things in life than fighting, killing and bottoms. Those of the British and German empires forgot about those other things.'

The analogy appealed to Daniel, and he began to cheer up a little. He gave Muriel a hurried explanation of everything that had been happening, leaving out the part about BC and Fox being from the future. By the time he had finished, they had reached Swanston Street.

'What about the bombs around the ceiling?' he now asked BC. 'Why did they not go off?'

'I cannot say,' replied BC.

Again Muriel put an arm around Daniel, and Daniel took care to press against her. Emily sneered, then turned back to BC.

'How is your stomach?' she said.

'Light damage, but I am still operational. I shall go to bed early tonight.'

BC needed to sit down by the time they reached the railway station. Daniel stood protectively beside her, but Muriel was holding his hand and stroking it a lot.

'I still cannot believe what I am seeing,' said Emily to BC, while looking directly at Daniel and Muriel.

'Daniel, I think you have learned that while it is easy to die for someone, it is a lot nicer to live for them,' ventured BC.

'Well, yes,' replied Daniel, putting an arm around Muriel as she pressed harder against him.

BC took out her small, black device and held it to her lips.

'BC reporting, serial KB7WCB0542,' she whispered. 'Request status. Trans.'

For some moments she listened, her eyes widening.

'What is that?' whispered Muriel to Daniel.

'A sort of telegraph,' he replied, and Muriel seemed to decide that this explained everything.

'Confirmed,' said BC into the device. 'Status, no target. Trans end.' BC shook her head then turned to Emily. 'Fox did nothing either.'

They were relieved to find that the train going south was almost empty. BC began to recover her strength as she looked out over the suburbs that the train was passing. Muriel unbuttoned BC's coat to check the bandages.

'Who put these stupid bandages on Liore?' muttered Muriel. 'No wonder there's bleeding.'

'The fuses, it must have been the fuses,' BC said as the train passed over the bridge spanning the Yarra River.

'Fuses?' asked Emily.

'Strings that burn slowly so that …' began Daniel.

'I know what fuses *are*!' snapped Emily before Daniel could betray her to Muriel. 'I mean why did they not work?'

'I have a theory,' said BC. 'The people who carried the bombs up and tied them under the ceiling probably did not know how to handle fireworks.'

'Or bombs,' added Daniel.

'On target. Perhaps some clumsy person picked up the bombs by the fuses, pulling them out of the explosives, but not the packaging.'

'I'll have to re-bandage you when we get home,' said Muriel to BC.

'There will be a terrible fuss when people take the packages down and discover what is really inside them,' said Emily. 'The Germans will still be blamed, because of the clues that have already been planted. The war may still happen.'

'We have done all that we can,' stated BC with finality. 'We did not stop the bombing. It was chance that did that. Perhaps chance will help us yet again.'

'So all that danger, those three deaths, they were all for nothing?' asked Daniel.

'A good soldier does not take credit for what someone else did. History has been different for the two hours past, that is all that I am sure of just now.'

'And you have not ceased to exist,' said Emily.

'Indeed, that too.'

'*History* is different?' asked Muriel.

'Don't ask,' advised Daniel, recalling how hard it had been to explain time travel to Barry.

All four of them were moving slowly and stiffly from their exertions of two hours earlier when they got out of the train at North Brighton Station. Barry the Bag was collecting tickets at the gate. There was nobody else on the platform.

'Barry, you will never guess what happened!' called Daniel, as they approached him.

'No bombs,' said Barry calmly.

'You know?'

'Yeah.'

'How?' demanded Emily, stamping her foot with annoyance as she stopped before Barry.

''Cause I flogged 'em with Lurker the Worker.'

'You what?' shrieked Emily.

'Well, ya told us all to work out plans, like some desperate stuff we was to do if everything came down in a pile of shit, so I did. I had a few words to Lurker the Worker, an' he dropped a message to Wreder the Writer.'

'Who is Lurker the Worker?' asked BC, closing her eyes, putting a hand to her head, and looking decidedly unsteady for the first time that day.

'Lurker the Worker is a horrid fat man who never

does any work,' explained Emily. 'Wreder the Writer is a railway stores clerk who writes out false dispatch notes – *and* once made some of Father's parcels disappear.'

'Yeah, but I got 'em back once I knew they was yer old man's!' protested Barry.

'Please!' barked BC. 'Everyone, let Barry continue.'

'Yeah, well … Wreder's a clerk, so I got Lurker to get him to check if any railway wagons had stuff that was to be unloaded onto carts goin' to the Exhibition Buildings this mornin'. I figured that they would keep the stuff safe like that until just before they wanted to use it. Anyway, he found a couple of dodgy lookin' wagons, so Lurker the Worker got back to me. Now Luker the Lurker was 'ere, havin' a beer with me old man and Lurker the Worker, it bein' a holiday, so –'

'Luker the Lurker?' asked BC as she sat down on a bench and put her face in her hands.

'He is a horrid thin man who works as a waiter during the day, and lurks about looking for things to steal at night,' said Muriel.

'Yeah, right, so I gives him a couple of me best artistic French postcards and asks him to mind the office and gate. Shoulda seen him when he saw those cards, he nearly choked on his beer!'

'Please, keep to the point,' prompted BC without looking up.

'Anyway, so Lurker the Worker and I took the next

train north and checked the wagons in Jolimont that Wreder the Writer told us about. One had bundles of stuff with fuses hangin' out and stuff about them bein' fireworks written on the wrappin'. I cuts one open, and there's big sticks of dynamite instead.'

'Nitroglycerine-based explosive,' said BC. 'Very dangerous.'

'Yeah, that's what Lurker the Worker said. Actually he said "Bleedin' 'ell, some cove's 'alf-inched a load of mining explosives!" Barry, Old Bagman, thinks I, here's an opportunity to dip into some wealth. "What's the worth?" says I. "Luker the Lurker would slip eighty quid", says he.'

'Speak courtly English, please,' said BC.

'Er, well, Wreder'd noticed that the papers for the wagon were missing stuff, like the owner's name. That's suspicious, so he'd not rat to the coppers. "Seller's market", says I.'

'Will someone please translate what he is saying?' asked BC.

'Barry stole a load of dynamite bombs disguised as fireworks from a railway wagon,' said Emily. 'He was told about them by some criminal who works for the railways. Barry then sold them to another criminal.'

'Who doesn't work for the railways,' added Daniel.

'Yeah, an' it was probably worth more tin than Luker the Lurker paid, but I wanted that load moved quick, no questions asked. When we got back 'ere,

Luker said certain mining operations of an unlicensed nature had an interest in cheap explosives with no questions asked, but he'd only pay sixty 'cause he'd have to hire a cart.'

'And you did this all by yourself?' asked Emily, starting to feel grudging admiration for Barry.

'Nah, Lurker the Worker helped me pull out the fuses – first time I seen him work, ya know? We put the load into a dogbox, then wrote FIREWORKS on some bags of cotton waste from another wagon and stuck the fuses in 'em. Then Wreder the Writer had the dogbox car shunted here.'

'Here?' gasped Daniel, Muriel and Emily together.

'Yeah, we unloaded, too. Packages store.'

'Will someone please translate again?' asked BC.

'The packages store currently contains enough dynamite to splatter this railway station all over Brighton and leave a very impressive crater,' said Daniel.

'Yeah, but only till Luker the Lurker turns up with a horse and cart.'

BC cast a glance in the direction of the packages store. Emily and Muriel hid behind Daniel as Daniel hid behind BC.

'How long?' asked BC.

'Half-hour, he said, but that was a while back, give or take. Ya know how it is when ya gotta find a Clydesdale and cart on a holiday, no questions asked.

We made sixty quid – that's twenty each for Lurker and Wreder, and twenty for me.'

'So Fox did not help?' asked Emily, still hardly able to believe what she was hearing.

'Nah, he's probably back at St Kilda, keepin' an eye out for German coves who really aren't Germans, and sketchin' things. I think he likes a bit of the old art, does our Foxy.'

Just then a cart drawn by an elderly horse crossed the railway tracks and came to a halt. The carter waved to Barry. BC glanced about hurriedly, then turned to the others.

'Emily, Muriel, stand guard with me, but keep your guns out of sight,' she said softly. 'Barry, Daniel, help whichever Lurker that is to load the cart.'

'But what will happen if I drop a package?' quavered Daniel.

'Try not to,' replied Barry. 'On second thought, mind the horse.'

Luker the Lurker and Barry the Bag were very skilled at loading carts with stolen goods in extreme haste. Within three minutes of the cart pulling up, it was rumbling away down Bay Street. In the distance they could hear the whistle of the train that had brought them there returning from the end of the line at Sandringham.

'Yeah, well, back to work, but twenty quid richer,' laughed Barry, obviously relieved that the danger was past.

BC gestured for Emily, Muriel and Daniel to stand beside her.

'Attention!' barked BC.

BC clicked her heels together and brought her fist across her chest in a salute. Emily and Daniel followed her lead, rather more clumsily. Muriel merely clasped her hands and looked awkward.

'We salute you, Barry Porter,' declared BC.

Barry suddenly looked astonished. He was used to either being ignored or shouted at. Being the centre of attention while not being shouted at or chased away was entirely outside his experience.

'Wot, me?' he managed.

'Yes,' said BC. 'Crew, stand easy.'

'But I was nowhere near parlyment, it was you lot out against the Germans.'

'Us?' snorted BC. 'Emily killed a spy, Daniel got shot defending me, I beat up a lot of people, and Muriel stopped us bleeding to death, but none of us did anything important. Barry, it was you alone who saved the future.'

'I ... you ... she *killed* a cove?' exclaimed Barry, going chalk white.

'We girls are very dangerous,' said Emily. 'We just don't boast about it like boys do.'

'I just bandaged people,' said Muriel huffily. 'I don't go shooting them.'

'But you have a gun,' Emily pointed out.

'Must be dreamin',' muttered Barry, his hands over his head.

'Had we followed your plan, Barry, nobody would have had to die,' BC explained.

Although it was clear that Barry was finding the revelations rather overwhelming, he snatched for what he hoped was a correct conclusion.

'So, I was all right, then?'

'The world will never know of it, but your plan was as clever as the Trojan Horse of the ancient Greeks, and those who were in the Charge of the Light Brigade were no braver than you,' said BC.

'Yeah, well, Miss Emily did tell me to think, so I did.'

'You thought even better than I could have,' Emily forced herself to admit.

'Cor, ta,' said the embarrassed Barry. He glanced south to the train that was now visible in the distance. 'Well, suppose I'd better get back to work.'

'No, wait here,' said BC, who then strode to the station office.

There was a crash and a shout of surprise, followed by several heavy thuds. Half a dozen beer bottles flew through the door and over the edge of the platform, where they smashed into splashes of foam and shattered glass between the rails. They were followed by Barry's father, who stumbled out onto the platform clutching his stomach. BC reappeared. Mr

Porter shuffled off to open the gates for the train.

'Barry, your father has very kindly agreed to mind the station by himself for the rest of the day,' announced BC. 'Emily, here are ten shillings. Why not take Barry back into Melbourne on that train? Show him the lights and decorations, and buy yourselves toffee apples. Daniel and I are going home. Muriel?'

'Somebody has to do your bandages properly,' Muriel declared to BC, although she was batting her eyelashes at Daniel.

The train pulled into the station.

'Hold your arm out!' Emily demanded, grasping Barry by the collar and stopping him as he made for the carriage.

''Ere, wot for?'

'So I can put my hand on it, like a lady with a gentleman. Now walk! Open the door – no! Get out again! You hold the door open for me while staying outside, *then* you get in and close the door behind us.'

'Is this meant to be a treat?' asked Barry, glancing forlornly at BC before closing the door.

The train chuffed out of the station.

'Barry the Bag, out on the town with Emily on his arm,' said Daniel in wonder as the three of them stood staring after the departing train.

'Am I meant to laugh or be sick?' asked Muriel, squeezing Daniel's hand.

'Barry Porter, he could have been the greatest

battle commander imaginable,' said BC, shaking her head.

'Yet in a way, he was,' said Daniel.

'I do believe you are right,' concluded BC. 'Barry the Bag commanding Lurker the Worker, Wreder the Writer, and Luker the Lurker. An uncoxed four! Yes, a small crew but an effective one.'

'Come along, heroes, bandage time,' said Muriel, tugging at Daniel's arm and BC's coat. 'The battle is over, so the nurse is in command.'

Two days later it was Saturday, and the six saviours of the century-to-come were gathered in a café near the river. Fox sketched other patrons while Emily tried not to choke on her first cup of coffee. BC sat scanning a newspaper for news of anything suspicious, and Daniel and Muriel sat holding hands. Barry was concluding the sale of an artistic postcard to someone with a bushy beard, who declared that he had come to Melbourne 'for the culture'. Deciding that she could force no more coffee down for the time being, Emily leaned closer to BC.

'BC, may I ask you two questions?' she ventured.

'No, I shall never tell anyone about last Wednesday night,' replied BC.

'Actually, that was not the question, but thank you.'

'Wednesday night?' asked Daniel and Muriel together.

'None of your business!' snapped Emily.

'Then what?' asked BC.

'Firstly ... well, it's not a question. I was waiting for some boy to come along and rescue me from my cage. You taught me that I could break out of that cage any time that I wanted to, without help from any boy. It was not easy, but it was not impossible.'

'True. We are all trapped in cages, yet all of us carry the keys. Finding the courage to use the keys, that is the hard part.'

'And second, your future ceased to exist when Barry stole the bombs that were supposed to destroy the Exhibition Buildings.'

'Yes.'

'Yet you and Fox did not cease to exist.'

'Obviously.'

'Why not?'

'Quite probably, it was a causality loop,' replied BC.

'Um, can that be explained to someone like me?'

'It was a future that happened, then looped back on itself and got bypassed by changed history.'

'Oh, but I thought you would sort of die, or, um, never have been.'

'Apparently time travel does not work like that.'

'So that was why you were not worried about changing your past?'

'No, I was indeed worried. I did not know that causality loops existed until two days ago.'

'Is this something to do with that time travel nonsense you tried to tell me about?' whispered Muriel to Daniel. Daniel nodded.

'So you thought you might die?' Emily asked BC, ignoring Muriel.

'Yes.'

'But weren't you afraid?'

'I am a soldier. Death is never far away for me. If some German boy had ashed me a hundred years in the future, would that be any worse? History looped upon itself. My future happened, at least until I vanished into the past. Now a new history will happen, and there will be no century with five world wars. My history has become a forgotten loop in time that did happen, but became closed off and bypassed. Fox and myself are all that is left of it.'

'But if your future has gone, you can never go back. Yesterday is different, now.'

'It was a bleak future in a mad world, Emily. I am content to stay here, and be part of this new time.'

Emily looked over at the others for a while, smiling, with her chin on her hands. Presently she tried some more coffee. Muriel squeezed Daniel's hand and smiled as Emily choked, then commenced a coughing fit.

'Fox loves artwork,' wheezed Emily to BC once she had got her breath back.

'A career as an artist is probably safest for him,' responded BC. 'At heart, he is a very gentle and sensitive soul. Muriel, that was very kind, introducing him to those teachers and other artists.'

'My pleasure. Anything for a friend of Daniel's.'

'Now then, there are some very stupid and dangerous men still on the loose,' said BC.

'Not to mention stupid and dangerous schoolgirl artists!' snapped Emily, glaring at Muriel.

'Enough!' said BC sternly. 'As I was saying, there are still several conspirators out and about. We really should deal with them.'

'Yes, indeed,' agreed Emily warily, and Daniel nodded too.

'Does that mean I have to keep carrying this silly gun in my knickers?' asked Muriel.

'Perhaps not. I have learned that cunning is vastly superior to firepower,' said BC, who now turned to Emily. 'What would *you* do?'

'You are asking *me*?' asked Emily in turn.

'I am not familiar with your times and society, so I need to learn from you. I may not agree with what you say, but I shall take it into account. Later I shall even ask Barry.'

Emily spread the papers that she had taken from the false policemen at the Exhibition Buildings. Nothing on them seemed to inspire her. She put them away again.

'Um ... first we need a plan,' she began. 'A plan based on what each of us does best.'

'Yes?'

'But we also need to be a team, to work together better.'

'Splendid idea.'

'So we shall hire a boat, a coxed four.'

'What?' exclaimed BC, her eyes suddenly wide.

'You are to be cox. Daniel can be stroke, he already knows rowing from school. Muriel shall be bow, and Barry and I can sit in the middle. What do you think of that? Fox can be the person who runs along the bank and shouts at us.'

'The coach,' said Daniel.

'Why?' asked BC softly.

'You are injured, you cannot row. Barry, Muriel and I need to become fit and coordinated.'

'I meant why should we learn to row together?'

'Because of what rowing does for people. We need to learn how to lock together as a perfect team, absolutely committed to winning and totally loyal to each other.'

'I think we are close to that already,' replied BC after considering Emily's words for a moment.

'That is my advice, Liore-BC. You may do with it what you will.'

BC folded her arms on the table, glanced at her crew, then looked across the river to the boatsheds.

Finally she stood up, called, 'Crew, to me!' and walked from the café. Emily explained what they were planning to Barry and Fox as they followed BC.

'Last time you and I got into a boat we nearly drowned,' Daniel pointed out to Emily as they walked across the bridge to the boatsheds.

'This time you will not stand up in the boat,' retorted Emily.

'Hope me bag doesn't get wet,' muttered Barry. 'Important items of a covert nature in me bag.'

'Confirmation, am coach, BC?' asked Fox.

'Kindly ask that in courtly,' ordered Emily.

'Ah ... Am I truly the coach, Miss Liore?' he said very slowly, pressing his hands against his temples.

'Thank you Fox, yes,' said BC.

'I still don't see why I have to row,' muttered Muriel to Emily.

And so the last surviving cadet battle crew of a British Empire that would never exist shakily steered their hired rowing shell out into the waters of the Yarra River in the late autumn of 1901. On the bank, Fox shouted instructions that went largely unheeded or misunderstood, and managed to keep up with the boat without even running. In terms of strength, skills and coordination, the crew was an ill-assorted collection, yet they were already absolutely loyal to each other and had won their first victory.